The Lone Piper and the Birds' Case

Kyuka Lilymjok

ISBN 978-9780-694-128

Published by:
Free Pen Publishers
10 Lachlan Close Maitama, Abuja

To my children Justice, Sunfair and Fairprincess

There is space for everyone
If everyone stays where he is
There is peace for everyone
If no one tries to eat
What belongs to another.

Chapter One

The sun was going down and life was gradually retiring from the numerous labours of the day. The western skies lighted by the setting sun looked like it was host to a wild bush fire. Flares of the fire at the edges they were strong bleached the sky white. The sun about to be swallowed by the sky was making an impressive exit.

Birds, insects, crickets and frogs were chirping, shrieking and croaking with the disharmony of a discordant choir. It was difficult to say whether they were celebrating the coming of night or lamenting the exit of day. For any of these creatures that night held prospects of food, peace and rest, the noise it was making was likely to be a celebration. For any of these creatures that night portended danger, its noise was likely to be a lament of the looming dark spectre.

A black-crested bird was flying home with his back against the setting sun amidst the noisy retreat of the day. There was a meeting he must attend towards the morning of the following day and he wanted to get home and sleep before the meeting which Welom the king of the birds of Kirkina savannah had called. In the air ahead of the black-crested bird was the spread of a kite all of water. This water kite always appeared before the black-crested bird every evening when the sun was setting like this. The black-crested bird called the water kite *the fairy of the evening sky*.

'The world is going to sleep and there is noise,' murmured the black-crested bird.

It was only a murmur, but *the fairy of the evening sky* heard it. *The fairy of the evening sky* not only heard murmurs and whispers, he could read the thoughts of a bird before they were expressed in words. So, he heard the murmur of the black-crested bird and replied, 'When the day wakes up tomorrow there will be noise. And the noise tomorrow morning will be by the same creatures making noise now.'

'It is with the day as it is with birds. When a bird dies, there is noise. When he is born, there is also noise,' said the black-crested bird.

'According to human beings, life is a creaking door. When you open it, there is a scream; when you close it, there is a scream,' said *the fairy of the evening sky*. 'The spirits of the dead are awake today. You can hear their drums in the air. Today must die for tomorrow to be born. Drums by the spirits of all the days that had died since you were born are calling on you the Lone Piper to play your pipe to mark the burial of today.'

The black-crested bird was a piper and was called the Lone Piper by every bird who knew him. Before him, his father was a piper. Before his father, his grandfather was also a piper. But neither his father nor grandfather was called the Lone Piper because both his father and grandfather played only before audiences. But the Lone Piper played both before audiences and alone. Indeed, he seemed to play alone more than before audiences. Than his father and grandfather, the Lone Piper had more zeal for his craft and clearly more genius. At a time it was lamented that birds were not as able in anything as those of old, the Lone Piper was hailed by all as a better piper than those he inherited the art from.

The Lone Piper was a middle-aged bird with a pleasant face and approachable manners. A smile that lit his face as much as the sun lights the earth was as much part of his face as his eyes and beak. When he was walking on the ground, he walked so lightly as to make it seemed he was walking in the air and not on earth. He had an unusually long beak for a black-crested bird. It was shaped in the form of a pipe and he used it as a pipe. From childhood, he had exercised it to produce melodies no pipe could. When playing his pipe, the air coming from his mouth and nose to produce the music of the pipe pushed his eyeballs out of their sockets as if to dance to the melody coming from the pipe. Often, he played not to entertain other birds, but himself. So alone in his nest, he played his pipe. Perched on a tree branch alone in the bush, he played his pipe. Alone in flight, he played his pipe. However, the quality of his piping while flying was not always as good as when he was on a tree branch or the ground.

When a bird was sick, the Lone Piper went to play for him. He did not play the pipe only when he got to the sick bird. He set out of his nest playing it up to the sick bird's nest. There was something magical about the music flowing out of his pipe. When he played his pipe on a tree or on the ground, birds stopped what they were doing and listened.

Those more moved by the music, moved closer to him to enjoy the melody more. For years, birds had heard the melody of his pipe, but never seemed to grow tired of it. This was partly because every day seemed to bring with it a new tune to the Piper and partly because of the soulful tone of his music. A song, often of ancient origin, was embedded in every tune the Piper played and almost every bird knew which tune was humming which song. For the Piper, the words of the song were vulgar. It was the tune that was refined that deserved the audience of his ears. In the home of the sick, whichever sick bird did not stir when the Piper arrived with his music was not likely to survive that sickness. His music had a way of making the very sick stirred in their sick-nests where they had lain for days without moving a limb, and some who had not talked for days to talk. Even after he was gone, a sick bird the Lone Piper had visited was likely to retain the vivacity the Piper brought to him for a long time. When there was a funeral ceremony, the Lone Piper was there to play a moving elegy. When he played in a funeral ceremony, birds wept not so much for the dead as out of the emotions the music from the Piper's pipe had stirred in them. When there was a wedding ceremony, the Lone Piper was there to remove the drab on life and give it colour and melody. When broods were hatched, the Lone Piper played his pipe to welcome them to the *toil* called life. Now *the fairy of the evening sky* all of water above his head, as always, was bidding him to play a dirge for the dying day and a song of hope for the day that would arise from its ashes.

The Piper lighted on a tree on the path of his flight to pipe. *The fairy of the evening sky* hung in midair to listen. The Lone Piper cleared his throat, which was the inner part of his pipe. It was a little damp and wonky. He cleared his throat again so that it would acquire its metallic edge that produced the gripping melody he cherished and believed his audience cherished. He was his first critic. If the melody coming from his pipe was not good, he knew by an empty feeling he had inside him and he strove to improve it. But if it was good, he knew by the excitement in his heart. And surely when he played the tune, it had on other birds the effect it had on him.

After he had cleared his throat and primed it for the task, he began to play. Immediately, his beak — the pipe, which had been lifeless, came into life. He was the god of the pipe. If he wanted it dead, all he needed do was to withdraw the breath he was blowing into it. If he wanted it alive, he breathed life into it as he was doing now and it would resonate with life. It would not only resonate with its own life, it would make other birds hearing its melody resonate with life.

Now tongues of a scintillating melody leapt from the pipe and filled the bush the Lone Piper was, spilling out into human neighbourhoods and beyond. Birds who heard it stopped whatever they were doing and listened. Life suddenly acquired a new pleasure, dignity and regard from those who thought it a pain and drudgery. Smiles replaced frowns and excitement ate up boredom. In a way, it was like the shot of cocaine with a hypodermic needle on the arm of a junkie; in a way, it was different. While a shot of cocaine leaves irritability, extreme anxiety, restlessness, paranoid psychosis and even heart-attack behind, the melody from the Piper's pipe left behind a refreshing sense of wellbeing and spiritual healing. Even the air appeared to be a happy bearer of the music coming from the Piper's pipe. It was only a tune, but it spoke to the souls of birds and men in a way no words could. It organized life into a beauty no word could express.

A man embroidering clothes nearby on hearing the melody of the Lone Piper, found his hands working a mesh of artistic designs he had not brought his hands to wrought. It was as if the melody was leaving soundtracks on the cloth, which his needle was following. Indeed, it was as if it had left unseen designs on the piece of fabric he was embroidering and he was merely tracing the designs left behind by the melody. A sculptor carving the sculpture of Ifidi the god of the mountains nearby, on hearing the melody, felt an enlivening sensation in his head. A painter painting, on hearing the melody, the painting brush in his hand which hitherto had felt like a bar of lead now felt like a leaf in his hand and he was swatting the wall with more grace and art. A man sitting and thinking why nemesis did not light upon evildoers now as was the case in bygone times, on hearing the Piper's melody, enjoyed a brainwave: It is not any supernatural being that brings nemesis, but common human resentment of evil. Therefore, where almost everyone in a community is evil, nemesis does not come to those who do evil in the way it would in a virtuous community where there is a shared goodness of mind and resentment of evil. Victims of evil or their relations in an evil community may *will* nemesis on an evildoer, but because they are doing so not from the point of communal resentment of evil, but from the point of personal grief, the communal *will* that would have brought nemesis to the evildoer would be lacking and so nemesis would not come.

Whenever the Piper was playing his pipe, he felt the whole of his being collecting around the pipe, which then became his heart pumping excitement to all parts of his body. Now as he played, his flesh seemed to dissolve into his lymph, which the pipe was tickling so pleasurably. Everything around him ceased to have life while he played. It was only he and the pipe that had life, which they were dispensing to those with ears to enjoy rhapsodies. Even his own life had no independent existence from that of the pipe. He might have been the one that first gave life to the pipe; but once it resonated with life, his own life became a mere *take* on the life of the pipe. He never stood still while playing. His head bent low, his eyes fixed on the ground before him, he shuffled his feet to and fro while his beak produced musical waves that rekindled and reaffirmed life as something worth being part of.

While the Piper played, *the fairy of the evening sky*
turned into a pool of water with only a mouth and
ears. When the Piper stopped playing, the pool of
water opened his mouth and spoke the words of the
Piper's melody:

One day we were sitting in the quiet of the
bushes
No one knew we would be visited
By *the merciless guest of tears*
That came riding a pale horse
On the cracked leaves of the dry season
Our eyes without blink stared in fear
At *the end of all promises* coming towards us
Our blood mixed with the fire from his breath
Was eaten by the pale horse which eats its own
shadow
But we shall live and laugh again
After *the guest of tears* had done his worse
Happiness and misery are all mixed in one
calabash
Like sand and millet; like air and dust
To see happiness again, look beyond the pale
horse
The smile hanging on the lips of *the last visitor*
Will wither like a lily planted in the desert.
Let those in this bush and about who hear my
song
Arise and laugh at the failure of *the ancient sadist.*

Chapter Two

The Lone Piper lived in Kirkina savannah with all manner of birds and animals. The Kirkina savannah which was once used to grow sugarcane had been left to lie fallow for many years. It has, in the course of the many years it was not cultivated, grown wild with tall grasses spanning its extent and thickets dotting its expanse. In the rainy season, the tall elephant grass seen from afar may make anyone who knew when the savannah was used for sugarcane cultivation but did not know the crop was no longer grown in the savannah, think he was seeing the sugarcane. In the dry season, the dry elephant grass united with the dusty atmosphere to give the savannah a ghostly appearance. A bird in flight that was of the colour of the dusty sky then might not easily be discernable from the sky.

From the branch of a tree or in his nest, the Lone Piper used to watch antelopes, zebras, giraffes and sometimes cows herded by Koton herdsmen grazing in the Kirkina savannah. From a tree branch in the forest, he sometimes watched a lion, a tiger, or leopard chasing an antelope or a zebra. Sometimes an antelope or zebra receiving an early warning of the presence of any of these predators was able to escape the fangs of the predator. But, often if the prey did not receive an early warning, the predator would pounce on it and tear it to pieces. Then the Lone Piper felt very sad and wished antelopes and zebras had wings in the air and not merely on land to flee their predators.

This year, a strange disease the birds had never known its kind was afflicting the savannah. Birds that first came to the savannah suspected strange red-crested birds that recently came to the savannah to have brought the disease. The symptoms of the disease were whitening of the plumage of an afflicted bird and eventual falling off of its beak. When the beak fell off, the bird would die. The tranquil and homely savannah was now unhomely and restive. Welom the king of the savannah had called for a meeting in the early hours of the morning to decide what to do in the face of the strange disease that was threatening to wipe out the whole birds of the savannah.

The decision to hold the meeting in the wee hours of the morning was informed by the king's desire to exclude the strange birds from the meeting. The meeting was to discuss them and it was therefore unwise to have them attend it. Because of its secret nature, notice of the meeting was passed in whispers to birds whose attendance was desired. Initially, the king had wanted to hold the meeting in the river that ran along the Kirkina savannah, but on consideration that some of the strange birds might be sleeping in the river, he decided to convene the meeting on the Honem mountain at the edge of the savannah.

The Lone Piper was one of the first birds that arrived the mountain for the meeting. He found Welom the king already seated. He was a solemn and reticent bird with penetrating eyes and a sunken neck. Some birds said he could recollect all he had said since he was born. Kings were chosen among birds of the savannah not on the basis of grandiose speeches by those seeking the office, but by their solemnity and reticence. The birds thought that loquacity was a vice that should not be found in the king. Lies were a taboo to the birds of the savannah. They saw lies and loquacity as neighbours. To them it was easy for a bird that talked too much to move from its nest of talking too much and enter the nest of lies.

Among the birds of the Kirkina savannah, it was the king who was always first at meetings. It was also the king that must first greet his subjects at any meeting because he is the servant of the birds. However, every decree of the king must be obeyed by his subjects. Refusal to obey the king's command in big or small matters such as the summon for this meeting was considered a sacrilege and any bird that committed this sacrilege would be banished from the savannah.

Perched on his royal spot, the king upon seeing the Lone Piper, rose and greeted him. The Lone Piper returned his greetings. Shortly after the arrival of the Lone Piper, the birds, which hitherto were arriving in trickles, began arriving in droves. Soon every bird that was invited was on top of the mountain. It was a bright moonlight night and the full moon rising from the east silhouetted the birds on the mountaintop in a manner Welom the king would not have desired.

The king observing that many birds had turned up for the meeting, rose up to speak to his subjects. But he did not say anything. Instead, he coughed and fell down. Many birds in panic rushed to him to help, but the king was beyond help. Welom the king of the birds was dead. Shocked and bewildered, the birds for a while were quiet. When shock and bewilderment began to lose their hold on the birds, lamentations tore the quiet night into shreds.

For some time Welom the king had not been seen much in public. There were rumours that he was sick. The king had not told anybody why he called the meeting. Some birds not knowing why the meeting was called, thought it was to discuss the health of the king. With the king dead without saying a word to them, some birds wondered if the king called the meeting to die before them? That was bizarre. It could not be. What killed the king? Was it the strange disease? The king had not been seen in public for a while now and so if his feathers were whitening not many birds would know. In the darkness of the night, it was difficult to tell the colour of the king's plumage. But if it was the strange sickness, the king's beak would have fallen off. They raised up the king and to their shock and indignation, the king's beak had fallen off. In their panic and bewilderment, they had not noticed earlier on that the king died without his beak.

There was a cry of vengeance by all birds on the mountain.

'We have been visited by visitors that are neither our relations nor our friends from distant lands,' said the Lone Piper.

'We have been visited by visitors we did not invite and they had come with a disease that removes your mouth before it kills you,' said the drummer.

'The beak of a bird is his hands and mouth,' said a bird. 'It is in fact the tail of a bird with which it drives away flies that cling to him.'

'With what will a bird eat food in the next world without a mouth?' asked another bird to the right of the Lone Piper.

'Happier are birds that died before the coming of this disease,' said some other bird. 'Long life sometimes is like scratching for food under a *cambam* tree. The longer you remain under the tree, the more the chances that your claws might stray into a trap.'

'Often long life is pushing your luck too far,' said another bird.

'It is difficult to contemplate a disease that can be crueller,' said yet another bird.

Other birds spoke as they were moved by the strange disease.

'The only respect this disease is showing us is that you die the moment your beak falls off.'

'Imagine living without your beak.'

'Imagine the king without his beak.'

'There can be no worse punishment.'

'There can be no worse indignity.'

'It is so awful.'

As the birds mourned their dead king, they heard the fluttering of the wings of birds in flight towards the mountain and later saw the outline of their mass as they descended on the mountain. It was the fire-crested birds. They were roosting on a string of *bembe* trees when they heard the lamentation of the birds on the mountain. In the quietness of the night, the lamentation of the birds was so dreadful and unsettling. Majority of the fire-crested birds without knowing what was responsible for the unsettling uproar had thought of fleeing from the noise. But a few of their number thought differently.

'The noise is by birds like us,' said one of the fire-crested birds that wanted them to investigate the cause of the noise. 'From the lamentation we hear, the birds mourning are in no position to harm us even if they are evil birds.'

'In fact, they sound like birds lamenting a great evil,' said another bird in support of the bird that just spoke.

'The birds crying may not be in a position to harm us, but what of the thing that is causing them to cry?' say a bird with an opposite view.

'That is what we may overlook to our harm,' said another bird. 'We can easily swap places with the birds crying out there.'

'It is clear the birds crying out there are not part of us,' said one other bird. 'There is no wisdom in being friendly in an unfriendly world or nice in an unnice world.'

'You have spoken my mind,' said another bird. 'Since we came here, every bird we met had treated us like lepers.'

'I will rather say like leprosy,' said another bird. 'And that is why we all huddled here every night though there is no space for one to stretch his legs or wings.'

'You are all right,' said a bird that wanted them to investigate the cause of the lamentation. 'But if we run away without knowing what we are running from, we might be running away from nothing. If that happens, we would be both foolish and cowardly. A fire-crested bird is not known for folly or cowardice.'

Almost every fire-crested bird was affected by the words of this bird and they all agreed to find out what was making the birds on the mountain to cry. At first, they did not know it was on the mountain the birds whose lamentation they had heard were. It was on their way to find out what was amiss that they discovered the mourning birds were on the mountain. This discovery made even the birds, which persuaded them to find out what had happened to begin to wonder if it was wise to go on with their mission. Birds do not sleep on top of the mountain. What could have carried the crying birds there to suffer the misfortune that was making them cry? They were about turning to head back where they were coming when they heard a bird on the mountain lamenting why their king would die like that after calling them to a meeting.

'So it is their king that is dead?' said one of the fire-crested birds. 'No wonder the uproar.'

'But why should their king call them to a meeting in an hour like this and on a mountaintop?'

wondered another fire-crested bird. 'It is ungood like to do so.'

'It may not be what we think,' said a bird behind the one that had just spoken.

'If they had no ungood intention towards us, how come none of us got invited to the meeting? We know our number. That number is not short of one where we stand now,' said a bird far off the edge of the crowd of birds.

'If the meeting was for an ungood thing towards us, they are having the first taste of their ungood intentions,' said some other bird.

'Maybe our fire crests had told them we are children of the sun,' said yet another bird. 'Any harm plotted against the sun while the sun is aglow would not hatch to the happiness of the plotter and that was why choice was made by them to meet in an hour like this. But as you can see, we are also children of the moon and that is why there is now confusion and lamentation in the enemy's camp. Fellow fire-cresters, let's go up that mountain. We have nothing to fear from the night as from the day. Let's go.' Saying this, the fire-crested bird that just spoke flew towards the mountain followed by the other birds.

Chapter Three

In one fluid but united formation, the fire-crested birds landed on the mountain while the Lone Piper and other birds were still wondering who the intruders were.

'We are here to know the illness making you cry in an hour you should be sleeping and to see if we have a wing to help,' said Flaming Eyes the leader of the fire-crested birds.

'You are the illness in our midst,' said the Lone Piper. 'The wing you would have used to help is lame with the disease you brought to us. Our king is dead.'

'Dead,' intoned Flaming Eyes.'

'Yes, dead,' repeated the Lone Piper.

Upon the Lone Piper repeating that the king was dead, a bird screamed as if it had been pricked with a needle.

'We should be careful how we scream,' said a bird near the bird that screamed. 'One's beak can easily fall off, screaming like this.'

'Those birds who talk too much had better beware. Their beaks can fall off,' said another bird

'Even those who don't talk are not safe. How much did the king talk and yet his beak fell off?' said some other bird.

'Those birds who eat too much had better watch it. They can leave their beaks in the camwood they peck for worms,' said a bird with a voice that sounded choky.

'The Lone Piper must watch his beak while piping. It can come off,' a bird said, smirking at the Lone Piper in the darkness of the night.

'But you know his beak so used to piping does not even know the Lone Piper uses it. So, he has nothing to fear,' said another bird.

'He has nothing to fear or we have nothing to fear. We benefit more from his pipe than he does,' said Longneck.

'It is unbad for you the Lone Piper to bare your mind to us,' said Flaming Eyes, butting into the exchange of the birds advising care in the use of beaks with the affliction of the strange disease. 'You have an unevil heart. You and your king might think we brought the disease that is disgracing birds before killing them, but you are unright. We have not even a feather, lest a wing in the disease. We are no less victims of it than you are.'

'But we did not know of this disease until your tribe arrived here,' said the drummer, standing to the left of the Lone Piper.

'You might be unwrong to say so,' said Flaming Eyes. 'But if you can remember, it was a month after our coming here that a bird in this savannah first caught the disease and it was not even a bird of our tribe, but of your tribe.'

The Lone Piper could remember all these. 'What you said Flaming Eyes is not untrue,' he said. 'But what do you mean to unprove by it?'

'What I intend to unprove by it is that we did not bring the strange disease afflicting this savannah. We may be strange birds in the savannah, it does not mean we are the carriers of strange plagues,' said Flaming Eyes.

'Disease mutates over time before it manifests,' said a black-crested bird. 'You could bring this disease to the savannah the day you came, but it would not show till much later.'

'According to men, disease is a thief. It does not knock on the door to tell you it is around. It sneaks in and only tells you it is around when it has settled in the pit of your stomach,' said the Lone Piper.'

'That is an unlie,' said a black-crested bird. 'That disease comes to steal life like a thief comes to steal property proves the unlie in that saying.'

'Rather than think we are responsible for this strange disease, I believe it is the aircrafts — the whirlybirds flying over the savannah that had shed this unheartly disease on all of us,' said Flaming Eyes.

Flaming Eyes' avowal caused a stir among the birds, particularly among the black-crested birds.

'But you have not being dying of the disease,' said a black-crested bird in a voice that sounded like it was coming from a hollow reed.

'You will not know we have been dying because you have never cared to know,' said Flaming Eyes. 'But the fact remains that we have also being dying like you and from the same disease. We have no king whose dead will create the sort of lamentation the dead of your king created. We are republicans that tolerate no king.'

'If you did not bring this disease, who brought it?' asked Madcap who had been too angry to speak since the fire-crested birds landed on the mountain.

'Like I said earlier, I believe it is the aircrafts – the whirlybirds that fly over the savannah that are spewing disease over our heads,' said Flaming Eyes. 'Yesterday I saw a low-flying aircraft dropping something near the river that runs along this savannah and I went to find out what it was. It turned out to be only an empty plastic bottle of water. But near the empty bottle of water, I saw under an undergrowth a white powdery substance I suspected was also dropped by an aircraft sometime ago. From its look, it couldn't have been dropped more than five or six weeks ago. As I stood watching the powdery substance, I had this feeling of nausea rising from the pit of my stomach to my mouth. Then I did not link the substance with the strange disease afflicting the savannah. But thinking of it now, I believe it is the cause of sickness and death in the savannah.'

'Liar!' cried Madcap, advancing threateningly on Flaming Eyes. 'Planes had been flying over this savannah before we were born. We had never gotten disease from them until you and your diseases-infested felons arrived and you open the same foul mouth from which you have been vomiting disease to our death to tell us such barefaced lies. What sort of fools do you take us for?'

'Who is this uncouth fellow?' asked Flaming Eyes of no one.

'I am the Madcap. I am wild as an unbounded wind.'

'I am Flaming Eyes and I was born to feed on Madcaps.'

Madcap sank his beak into Flaming Eyes neck and Flaming Eyes crying out in pain kicked out at Madcap. The Lone Piper moved in to separate the two fighting birds, but as he was driving himself between the two combatants, a fire-crested bird said, 'today, these lousy black-crested birds would know that the fire on our heads can burn the coal on their heads. We are children of the sun and our fire crests were given to us by the sun.'

Hearing this, the Lone Piper was gripped by a blinding anger and flung himself on the fire-crested bird that spoke the provocative words. Every black-crested bird on seeing the Lone Piper seen as a bird of peace attacking the fire-crested bird that had insulted their tribe, flung himself on any fire-crested bird near him.

The fight on the mountaintop raged on till daybreak. It was a fearful sight. Birds pecked each other violently with intent to kill. Most of the pecking was from the neck upward where a violent peck would be fatal. Using their talons, birds tore open the stomachs of birds they were fighting, spilling their guts on the mountain. Though the moon was shining, being night, fire-crested birds and black-crested birds attacked and killed their fellows in the wild melee on the mountain without knowing. By daybreak, not less than two hundred birds had been killed by fellow birds. Fighting in the night, the horror of what they were doing was largely unseen by them. But with the coming of daylight, when birds lucky not to have been killed saw the carnage around them, they all fled the mountain in terror of what they saw. Only the Lone Piper who had also survived the fight was left on the mountaintop. Standing in the midst of the carnage, the Lone Piper began to pipe a moving elegy:

> The beaks we used to feed life
> We have used to feed death
> Death like a savage glutton
> Is feasting on our beaks
> Without the courtesy of gratitude
> How better off we would have been
> If we had all lost our beaks
> To this strange disease before today
> When we fed death so gleefully
> We have answered the call of the earth
> Against the voice of the sky where we live
> We have sowed our blood and tears
> On the infertile land of suspicion and hate
> Where we will not reap cheer and laughter
> But more blood and tears
> When the goat vents its frustration on the sheep
> He sows cheer and laughter for the hyena
> Our beaks are so full of blood

Wheat and barley will not sprout
Where we sowed our blood and tears
But weeds, pests and the whirlwind
Shall spin into each other like a tangle
nest
Until they strangle all of us
Our talons so full of our own flesh
Make us dizzy in the head and giddy on
our feet
If the mere sight of what we did make
us sick
How much the thought of what we
did?
Shame, shame where are you?
Come and save us from pride
Sun glare more on our dark hearts
So that we see the ungood lying there
So that we see wounded care bleeding
there
And we will flee our hearts
The way we fled this mountain.
Heaven – mercy, mercy, mercy
Mercy for us and mercy for those we
killed.

All the surviving birds on hearing this moving elegy wept. One by one they returned to the mountain where the Lone Piper was repeating his elegy over and over again. The mountain was soaked with the blood of their fallen members. They stood in dread of what they had done and in revulsion of the blood dripping from the mountain. In the dreadful silence that gripped the birds at the foot of the mountain, the voice of the Lone Piper all alone on the mountaintop reciting his elegy soaked the air not like the blood that soaked the mountain, but like lather-rich water soaking dirty clothes. It filled the early morning air like the song of a nightingale recreating the world in its own image. From the foot of the mountain, the Lone Piper no longer looked like a bird to the rest of the birds, but like the image of a god. When he began to speak of the god-awful things they did in the night, there was a cry from the foot of the mountain that while Welom was the king of black-crested birds, the Lone Piper was more than the king of all the birds of the savannah. He was the *Heart of all the birds* of Kirkina savannah who would do whatever was his bidding. The birds spoke severally.

'He is most knowledgeable among birds.'
'He is wiser than any bird.'
'He is sober and thoughtful than any bird.'
'He has the armoury to deal with the enemy.'
'Life and beauty lie in blending opposites,' said the Lone Piper. 'To create and sustain the world, opposites were needed. To give beauty to the world, opposites must live side by side. We add to the beauty of the world if fire-crested birds and black-crested birds live together in harmony. I am not talking of the law of dualism here, but the principle of fulfilling the demands of beauty. Fire-crested birds and black-crested birds are brothers. Why then should we do this to ourselves!' he cried. 'We must have a law against *ourcide* — killing ourselves. Even

primitive humans who got the idea of flying from us have laws against *ourcide*. We should do better than them. Humans must aspire to be like us in laws as they aspire to be like us in flight. 'Henceforth this mountain would be called *the mountain of blood*,' he went on after a momentary pause. 'It would only be mounted if we desire to spill the blood of an enemy. Flaming Eyes is dead. But before his death, he said something we must not allow to die with him. He said the fire-crested birds who are our brothers from distant lands did not bring the strange disease afflicting us in this savannah, but the disease was dropped here by ungood human beings in an aircraft. We must investigate his allegation and if found to be true, we must avenge him and all birds that lost their lives because of this ungood act. On this same mountain that we spilled the blood of our brothers, we will spill the blood of unkind human beings if we find Flaming Eyes allegations to be true. Without wasting time, we will now all move to the river where Flaming Eyes said the powdery substance was dropped and see if there is such substance. If there is such substance that provokes nausea in us, woe-be-tide whoever dropped it.' Saying this, he flew off the mountain towards the river. The birds at the foot of the mountain followed him behind. Black-crested birds were happy their own was now lord of the savannah. Fire-crested birds were happy their own was respected by the *Heart of the birds* who was a black-crested bird.

Chapter Four

It took the Lone Piper and the other birds a long time to find the powdery substance Flaming Eyes said was dropped by men in an aircraft. It was hidden under a shock of leaves of undergrowths very close to the water of the river. It was surprising how despite so well-hidden Flaming Eyes was able to see the powdery substance. 'But that was why he was Flaming Eyes,' said one of the birds. 'His eyes were like flames that lit everywhere so that he could see what other birds could not.'

Evidence that the powdery substance was dropped from above was on the leaves of undergrowths the substance was under and the leaves of taller trees it passed through. A faint feeling of nausea was rising from the stomachs of all birds to their throats. With the substance so near the water, there was no doubt that some of it had entered the water, which was the water they drank. Of course, it was in the air they breathed and that was why they were now having nausea. So hidden, a bird with a poor sense of smell could stand near the powdery substance for a long time and inhale its toxic fumes in the air without knowing.

'Once more a god-awful thing has been done by ungood human beings to unbad birds!' cried the birds in the river, all scampering to fly away.

Far away from the river, the Lone Piper flying in front of the birds lighted on a tree. All the other birds lighted on the same tree.

'We must somehow find something to cover up the poison in that river so that it is no longer carried by the air to feed us with death or enter the water we drink,' said the Lone Piper. 'When the rainy season comes, whether we are still alive or dead, flood will carry away the toxin from our neighbourhood.'

'That is the unwrong thing to do,' said Longneck. Other birds nodded their assent. They went about looking for what to use to cover the powdery substance and were lucky to find a big leather floating in the air. After finding the leather, they gathered twigs they would use as screws to hold the leather over the substance. When they were ready to go back to the river, they used leaves to cover their mouths and noses to reduce the smell of the substance they would inhale. The leather was carried by the Lone Piper and Longneck. They held it with their beaks and flew towards the river with the leather fluttering between them. When they got to the river, they quickly threw the leather over the white substance, screwed it to the ground with the twigs they came with and fled the river again back to the tree the decision was taken to cover up the powdery substance in the river. This tree was to be later christened by the Lone Piper as *the tree of decision* where important decisions affecting birds of the savannah were to be taken.

'We have now performed a very important task,' said the Lone Piper. 'Those who do not die now would enjoy the benefit of our labour today. For three weeks, we will hang this matter on this tree. If after three weeks, there is a decline in sickness and death in the savannah, we will know where sickness and death have been coming to us. But if there is no decline in sickness and death, we would have to look further for the source of our affliction. Long live the birds of Kirkina savannah!' he saluted the birds.

'Long live *the Heart* of Kirkina savannah!' cried the birds in one voice. The birds dispersed to apply themselves to their various persuasions. The Lone Piper followed birds that had lost relations in the fight to their nests to condole them. The *Heart of the birds* was indeed the *Heart of the birds.*

Though he was now the *Heart of the birds*, the Lone Piper went on playing his pipe to the delight of all birds. Such sport instead of diminishing his esteem with the birds, enhanced it. What was more, if the birds truly wished their *Heart* long life, he had to go on playing his pipe; for a day without playing his pipe made him sick.

After condoling birds on the day following the night of the mayhem, the Lone Piper perched on *the tree of decision* and played the tune of a song the words of which every bird knew. The song was an ancient song that spoke of how good and kind life once was:

> In those days of ease and plenty
> All that a bird needed was by his nest
> Worms to eat, water to drink
> Grasses for the making of nests
> Were all within the ease of birds
> Birds envied each other

But did not fight over worms, water or
grass

When birds smiled with their beaks
There was a smile in their hearts
The smile on their beaks
Was a report of the smile in their
hearts

Today the things birds need
No longer abound within their ease
Fear, toil and care are now by the side
of every bird

Now birds smile with their beaks
When their hearts are aching with
worry and fear

Birds have lost the touch of fellowship
Which a bird shared with his fellow
bird

In the fierce struggle to snatch food
From the beaks of their neighbours
Birds have lost the touch of care
That is why life has become a long
funeral

Without a ceremony of songs
The tree of love has withered
Under the drought of what to eat
Birds are cooling towards each other.
As hunger hots up between them.

Around the Lone Piper, there was an atmosphere
of sadness and joy. Beyond him, his melody was
creating a climate so sorrowful as to be
heartbreaking and so genial as to be soul healing.

Like push-brooms, the melody of the Piper pushed back worries and unhappiness in many birds and like dykes, halted the undertows.

A human being passing by and hearing the piping by the Lone Piper would have imagined a piper and a drummer in the land of men. When the Lone Piper danced to his melody, a passing human being would have seen in his mind a drummer with his drum hanging on his shoulder while his sickle-shaped stick rammed on the drum moderated by the palm of his left hand resting on the edge of the drum partly to give balance to the drum and partly to moderate its shrillness whenever the stick fell on it. He would have seen the central area of the skin where the stick frequently fell looking whiter than the periphery. Looking at the portion of the skin the stick had worn out to a faded white hue, he would have been reminded of a portion of a carpet that was treaded on more often than other parts of the carpet or indeed a bush path created by human feet. He would have seen a drummer in a stooping posture, rooted on one spot, one leg thrust forward, the other standing on toes like a sprinter ready for the *start* shout. While beating his drum, the drummer of human imagination would occasionally swing round without lifting a foot from the ground. Though his feet and other parts of his body would not be moving, his head would be snapping up and down in tune with his drumbeats and pipe rhythm – sometimes snapping his head so vigorously that pity would be heard for his neck that bore the brunt of his excitement. But while the drummer would be standing still, the piper that always moved with him would be dancing round him as he blew his pipe — the majesty of his dance-steps flowing from the symphony and rhythm of his music.

This afternoon, after playing the pipe to the satisfaction of his cheer and melancholy, the Lone Piper felt condoled himself. 'Music is like sleep,' he murmured, looking relaxed and satisfied. 'It is so restorative of life. Whenever I finish singing, it is like I have woke up from sleep. Music is so important to life that though whales were not given speech, they were given music.'

Chapter Five

The night after the mayhem was a terrible night. It was perhaps the most awful night the Lone Piper and any other bird in Kirkina savannah had ever gone through and may ever go through. The eerie and esoteric lamentation of the spirits of dead birds filled the air making every bird snuggled to the walls of its nest in fear. The fluttering of the wings of invisible birds hard by, their pitiful and spine-tingling screams turned the night into a massive horror chamber. It was like every dead bird was waiting for nightfall to come to life again.

The moon rising towards dawn, the early part of the night was pitched dark. The Lone Piper alone in his nest could hear strange, haunting noises coming from *the mountain of blood*. The noise of shrieking insects, croaking frogs and shrilling crickets mingled with the strange and frightful noises coming from the dead to give the night a horrid character that left even the brave lame with fear. Perhaps the frogs, insects and crickets frightened by the lamentations of the dead were shrieking and croaking out of fear. Each creature dead or alive seemed to be either lamenting a great evil that has happened or may happen later in the night. Birds killed during the mayhem moved from bemoaning the evil they had suffered to screaming their agony so that heaven would do something.

Ruddycheeks whose nest was not far from that of the Lone Piper could not sleep in his nest. Horrid images making fearful noises fluttered about his nest as if they would tumble it to the ground. The eyes of an owl without the body of the owl wafted past his nest like two ice chips floating on water. Ruddycheeks screamed. Unable to sleep in his nest and unable to stand the fright around the nest, he kept running to the nest of the Lone Piper which could barely take one bird. Each time he came, the Lone Piper very much in need of assurance himself, would assure him that no harm would befall him and so he should go back to his nest. On his third coming, the Lone Piper told him that as he could see his nest was just the size of the nest of a black-crested bird, which could barely accommodate one bird. If the nest were bigger, the two of them could have passed the night together. But if they tried to do so in this small nest, they would end up pulling it apart with their wings and legs. And it was not easy making a nest these days as it was in years gone by.

'But you are the *Heart of the birds* of this savannah; you can ask the birds to make a new and bigger nest for you,' said Ruddycheeks.

'Why are you talking as if you are a chimpanzee?' said the Lone Piper. 'Well, I won't blame you. The fear of this night can make any bird to even forget it is a bird. If not, you know as the *Heart of the birds* I have no power to ask any bird to make a nest for me. It's only chimpanzees whose chief has such powers.'

'This night can provoke the worse thoughts in any bird,' said Ruddycheeks. 'Else, how could such a thought cross my mind?'

'It wasn't even a thought,' said the Lone Piper. 'It was the ravings of your fears. Please, go back to your nest. It is well.'

'It is well and the air is full of these dreadful noises and I am shivering like an old monkey rain has beaten? If you say this is well, how would things be if it is sick? I am going nowhere. I will rather sleep beside your nest than go back to my nest to face the horrid images that keep looming before me.'

'I mean to say it will be well,' said the Lone Piper. 'You will not sleep outside your nest. Go back to your nest and see what would happen.'

'I have no nest to go back to,' said Ruddycheeks.

'What happened to your nest?' asked the Lone Piper in a voice that conveyed shock to Ruddycheeks.

'The spirits of the dead have taken over my nest,' said Ruddycheeks, mournfully.

'You know as well as I do that that is not true,' said the Lone Piper in a tone that did not carry his feelings. Before Ruddycheeks said his nest has been taken over by spirits of the dead, he had had the haunting feeling of spirits of the dead being in his own nest with him. But he would not confess his feelings to Ruddycheeks. 'You have to go back to your nest,' he said persuasively. 'I assure you there are no spirits of the dead in your nest. If they are not in mine, why should they be in yours?'

'It is not a matter of you assuring me *Heart of the birds*,' said Ruddycheeks. 'It is a matter of what I know I will find in my nest when I go back there.'

The reply of Ruddycheeks confirmed the fears of the Lone Piper that his voice did not carry the conviction needed to allay the fears of Ruddycheeks. His voice must carry the conviction needed to persuade Ruddycheeks to go back to his nest. The times called for bravery among the birds and what was happening this night offered a rare opportunity for the birds to begin to show the bravery that would be required of them in the days ahead.

'If there are spirits of the dead in your nest, it is because you ran away,' said the Lone Piper. 'Other birds who spirits of the dead had tried to chase away from their nests, but who refused to flee, the spirits had had to leave them alone and go chasing birds they can frighten away. The days ahead, Ruddycheeks, I tell you have no place for lily-livered birds, but for birds that can look death in the face and laugh, else rats will be seizing worms from the beaks of birds and making fun of them as their spite dictate. You have to go back to your nest and stay together with the spirits of the dead there if they will not respect your presence and flee. That is what the times demand of you, not me.'

Ruddycheeks suddenly remembered that no bird refused to do as he was told by his *Heart*. So, he went back to his nest as urged by the Lone Piper, though he was still possessed by fear.

Without prelude, the Lone Piper in a rare burst of energy and fervour began to play a tune on his pipe that no bird had ever heard and would never hear again. In a meditative, sorrowful tune that connected all birds with the life before them and the life after them; a tune depicting the thoughts and dreams of every bird for a world free of misery, agony and death, and a world full of laughter, happiness and prosperity, he appealed to all birds to bolster their faltering courage. In a solemn and reverent tune, he appealed to the aggrieved spirits of the dead in the air, on *the mountain of blood* and on the trees with them to have mercy, to know that they would be avenged when it was known who brought the disease that led to the massacre on *the mountain of blood.*

Suddenly every screaming creature fell quiet. Birds felt into a trance and the whole savannah came under a healing influence the world was said to come under when the Buddha was born. As abruptly as the Lone Piper started piping, he stopped. But most creatures that were screaming were then asleep. However, some of them did not sleep long. Haunted in their sleeps by nightmares, they woke up screaming again. One of them, Horsevoice, flew to the Lone Piper for refuge from the horrendous night.

'See, see, see! It is pursuing me with a long beak and the claws of an eagle to tear open my stomach,' he cried, stumbling into the Lone Piper's nest.

'No one is pursuing you,' said the Lone Piper. 'It is only your own fears that are pursuing you.'

'But look at it going away because I am with you!' screamed Horsevoice.

'I tell you, you are only suffering from hallucinations bred by your fear. No monster is pursuing you.'

'It is so, so terrible,' panted Horsevoice. 'I have no pair in my memory to what I saw. And the monster sits in my mind refusing to leave though it has disappeared from my vision.'

'That is the problem,' said the Lone Piper cuddling Horsevoice with his wing. 'You carried your fears into your sleep and that is why you cannot sleep. I can appease the marauding spirit in the air to allow you to sleep, but only you can persuade the frightful monsters in your mind to allow you enjoy the sleep that has been secured for you.'

'You mean I went to sleep with monsters in my mind?'

'You just said so yourself,' said the Lone Piper.

'The monsters I saw before I went to sleep left my eyes and mind when you began to play your pipe. It is the monster that I saw now that is refusing to leave my mind,' said Horsevoice, snuggling closer to the Lone Piper.

'Maybe it did not leave as you think, but merely went to sleep the way you did when I played my pipe,' said the Lone Piper. 'But it did not sleep long. It woke up soon after and woke you up.'

Horsevoice did not say anything. It seemed what the Lone Piper said made sense to him.

'You can see why you cannot sleep?' said the Lone Piper, patronizingly. 'Listen; how much noise can you hear now? Very little; and the little noise you hear is the noise of birds like you who went to sleep with monsters in their minds that would not let them sleep. Heaven and hell if you don't know are in the mind. Go back to your nest and try to chase away the monster in your mind and you will sleep.'

With much reluctance, Horsevoice went back to his nest. By the time he was back in his nest, many other birds had been woken up by nightmares and the savannah was once more becoming charged with fearful noises. The Lone Piper began piping once more and soon all was quiet again.

'I will use my beak to pipe peace and happiness into the hearts of all birds,' said the Lone Piper, feeling at peace with himself. 'After all, it was for this reason I was born. I was sent to deliver birds from the misery of the world. I was born to be the messiah of birds and I will deliver them with the melody from my pipe which no black-crested bird has the like of.'

Chapter Six

Like most birds had expected, within the three weeks the Lone Piper set for the birds to observe whether there was a decline in sickness and death after they covered up the powdery substance in the river, there was a marked reduction in the incidence of the dreadful disease and the deaths it brought. On the completion of the two weeks, the Lone Piper called a meeting on *the tree of decision*.

'The three weeks we set for our observation are over, what have we observed?' asked the Lone Piper when all the birds had assembled. He knew there was a drop in the death of birds, but let this fact comes from his subjects.

There was a chorus of almost all the birds that sickness and death had gone down. As a matter of fact, only two birds had died since the white substance was covered up. These two birds were suspected to have contracted the disease before the substance was covered up.

'We now know from where death was coming to us,' said the Lone Piper, with a grim look no bird had ever seen on his face. 'Humans flying in aircrafts over our beloved savannah have been the cause of our sickness and death by the toxic substances they dropped in our precious savannah. They have brought human flu to the savannah. Human flu we all know is the deadliest disease. Now is the moment of decision,' he said and looked about him for affirmation, which came instantaneously.

Before calling the meeting, the Lone Piper had not thought and decided what the birds would do if there was consensus that aeroplanes were the cause of the strange disease afflicting the savannah. What to do in that event he felt was a matter for the birds to decide, not him as their leader. All he would do was to give direction and he proceeded to give direction by asking the birds what to do.

'What can we do to such a powerful enemy?' a bird wondered in despair.

'Most things do not have the power we think they have,' said Longneck. 'But if we think they have such powers, they will have them.'

'Human beings have no wings to fly,' said Beakybeaky. 'That means they are not as powerful as some of us think. If we can deny them the use of aircrafts, they cannot fly.'

'We must exclude human beings from the air,' said Bignose with a lot of zeal.

'Hirrrrr,' many birds shrieked in approval.

'The skies are made for birds not for human beings,' said the Lone Piper. 'Human beings were never intended to fly. Flying, brassfeathers, is the privilege of birds. Brassfeathers, there are two types of beings on earth: glow-worms and mort beetles, civil and rude beings. Birds are glow-worms and civil. That is why they have the privilege of flying, walking on land and even on water, to extend civilization to the whole world. Men are mort beetles and rude beings. That is why they can only walk on land, which lacks the refinement of the air and the sea. If they must walk on water or in the air, they have to depend on clutches. That is why I call them *clutches-dependent cripples*. We have to reform them by killing them,' he said in a high-pitched voice and paused for a moment before continuing. 'No one is reformed without blood. It is the blood shed on *the mountain of blood* that reformed us. Right from the time of our fathers when men started flying in aircrafts, we had watched the development with increasing apprehension and distaste. Sometimes in the course of their flight, they had killed innocent birds in the air – a home that is supposed to be exclusively theirs. Vibrations they create in the air during flight have caused the sickness and death of many birds. They deliberately built the engine of the aircraft outside the aircraft to feed us with toxic fumes while they enjoyed the flight. They eat the corn and throw the cobs at us. All these must stop. We have suffered many other discomforts in the air because of having to share it with primitive humans without hitting back. But now that there is a deliberate attempt by them to poison the air with human flu, birds must wake up from their slumber before it is too late. For any bird yet to know it, the world today is a wicked, wicked web spun by bloodsucking spiders to suck the living blood of any fly that strays into it. Today, the world has no place for a bird that would not insist on his rights. Brassfeathers of Kirkina savannah, there are no such values as morality and immorality in life that permit or forbid action. The only inhibition of action I know of is cowardice. The only spur of action I know of is courage. A bird is either a coward or courageous. When a bird is a coward and so could not take action, he would say he is a moral bird that would not do a thing that is immoral. The bird that is brave and can do the thing, he would call an immoral bird. Cowardice has always been a cheap blackmailer. We must attack those attacking us. Those killing us, we must kill. We were in the air before they intruded into it. We can exclude them from it and we will exclude them from it. We will start the war against all aircrafts in the airports. Birds are not strangers in airports. They go there to feed on grasshoppers. So, having access to a plane on ground in an airport is not such a difficult thing for birds. If we are seen as part of the airport community just as the grasshoppers are, our sight in the airport alarms or alerts no one. So, we can easily have access to a plane. The excreta of the *minta* bird is very corrosive. They would go and excrete inside the engines of aircrafts in the airport. Luckily for us, the jet engine and the turbo-prop engine are outside and easy to get into if not covered. So, the *minta* birds would excrete inside the engines and leave the battle of crashing the aircrafts to their excreta. Check valves – the so-called one-way-valves in the engines that only allow things out of the engines, but do not allow anything in would be destroyed by the excreta of *minta* birds, which would find its way into the engines. In the course of two days or so the engines of a plane that have been excreted into would fail in mid-flight and that would be that.'

There was a loud din of approval of this declaration of intention.

'That is not all,' said the Lone Piper, looking pleased with himself. 'From the airports we will bring the war to this savannah. In no distant time, we will declare this savannah a Bermuda triangle for all planes flying across it. Any aircraft passing here will not suck air into its lungs, but death. I am familiar with the art of aerobatics. We shall develop the art of aerobatics to such a level that we can outfly and outmanoeuvre any aircraft in the sky.'

'What is aerobatics?' many birds wanted to know.

'Aerobatics is flying faster than is usual and making unusual manoeuvres in the air,' said the Lone Piper. 'It is flying with an extraordinary speed and making stunning manoeuvres in the air that awes any bird perceiving it.'

'Even by description, this sounds thrilling,' said Bignose.

'There is no doubt that it is more thrilling in experience,' said the Lone Piper. 'That is why human beings had developed the art. Anything that has fun in it, you can trust human beings to want to have a taste of it – their everyday lives on the ground being such bores.'

'But how do you come to know the art of aerobatics?' asked a bird.

'In the skies over Hundo airport in Dinato, it is almost a weekly sport,' said the Lone Piper. 'There, aircrafts perform magical manoeuvres in the air that racing cars cannot perform on the ground.'

'I can hardly wait for the training in aerobatics to start,' said Beakybeaky, full of excitement.

'Yet, you have to wait,' said the Lone Piper with a faraway look. 'I have to train myself in the art first before I can train anybody.'

For six weeks after this discussion, the Lone Piper was not seen in Kirkina savannah. No bird knew where he had gone to, but every bird knew he had gone to a new land to learn the art of aerobatics. But for the fact that the birds knew the Lone Piper would not want to be seen by human beings learning the art of aerobatics, some birds would have said he was in Dinato. But the birds knew that the last thing the Lone Piper would want was to be seen by human beings practicing the art of aerobatics. If he had to go away from the savannah so as not to be seen by fellow birds learning the art, he would resent the more human beings watching him learn the art.

During the six weeks the Lone Piper was away from the savannah, birds scanned farther horizons for signs of the Lone Piper in the air, but there was no sign of him. Some birds even flew far in search of him, but did not find him. The Lone Piper must have gone very far for his training the birds thought. A bird shot by a hunter in mid-flight was, while falling down, seen by some birds as the Lone Piper in aerobatic display; but the birds that flew to where the bird had fallen were disappointed to find it was not the Lone Piper, but a bird that had been shot dead.

When expectations of the Lone Piper returning to the savannah were beginning to turn to fear that he might not have gone for training in the martial arts of aerobatics, but something bad might have happened to him, he returned, rather dramatically. He looked athletic and leaner than he was before he left.

'Where have you been all these weeks?' asked Longneck.

'Across the seas,' said the Lone Piper.

'No wonder,' said Longneck. 'We have looked for you everywhere without any sign of you. You should have hinted to at least a bird where you were going. We were afraid something ungood had happened to you.'

'When I want to ensure that I carry out an action, I first express it to other birds,' said the Lone Piper with a look of fulfilment. 'When I do so, I have to carry out the action, if for nothing, to save my face before the birds I had talked to. When I said I will train other birds in the fine art of aerobatics, I have to fulfil that promise to remain honourable in the eyes of the birds. So, I had to go and acquire the skills of aerobatics. I needed to be all alone to concentrate on my training. So, I left quietly to train in Kansand Island. Now I am back; my wings are rippling with the most quintessential art on earth.'

'You will always remain an enigma to other birds,' said Longneck, looking at the Lone Piper admirably. 'Queak, quik, queck!' Longneck let out a cry that called all the birds of Kirkina savannah to assemble.

The birds, as if they were waiting for the cry, immediately assembled around the Lone Piper and Longneck. They were all surprised to see the Lone Piper who some were beginning to fear was dead.

Like Longneck, they told the Lone Piper how they felt about his absence.

'I am your *Heart*; if I die, you die,' the Lone Piper said, jocularly.

Some birds laughed. But Ruddycheeks did not. For him, it was a grim joke pregnant with meaning. How could they have made the Lone Piper the *Heart of the birds* without thinking of the grave implications? Emotions never serve anyone well, he thought. The decision to make the Lone Piper the *Heart of the birds* was taken in a moment of wild emotions when the minds of the birds were ruled by their hearts. Now this was the result.

'I went away quietly to learn the art of aerobatics,' Ruddycheeks heard the Lone Piper saying, 'and I have learned the sublime art and can teach other birds the art,' he went on excitedly.

While the birds were still marvelling at what the Lone Piper had said, he shot into the air at a dizzying speed looping, rolling and stalling in midair before swooping down to land on the very spot he stood at the centre of the assembly of birds.

The Lone Piper's performance was shocking, stunning and too fleeting for some of the birds to follow.

'Incredible!' cried Longneck.

'What!' exclaimed Beakybeaky.

'Terrific!' cooed Bignose.

'Impossible!' shrieked Ruddycheeks.

'Very possible,' said the Lone Piper. 'If I can do it, any other bird can, and before your eyes I have done it.'

Some birds were happy that a new way of flying which the Lone Piper called the fine art of aerobatics was now within their reach. Other birds were afraid they would never be able to learn the art. To these birds, the Lone Piper was a magician and the performance he had enacted before them was a piece of magic.

The Lone Piper sensing the dismay among this group of birds told them not to despair. The art of aerobatics would be taught gradually, deliberately and installmentally in such a way that every bird would in the end be a master of it.

Chapter Seven

To help the birds learn fast the art of aerobatics, the Lone Piper began by explaining to them what he called the four foundation stones of aerobatics. These are the loop, the roll, the stall-turn and the spin. In the loop, a bird already high up in the air drops to a lower altitude and then swing up in an arch-form. While dropping, the bird frees himself of the labour of flapping and stretching his wings to remain in the air. It is like the harvest of the labour of climbing into the air. The roll is either a wingtip down rotation or a wingtip flat rotation. High up in the air, a bird can go into a roll in a cycle. Using the roll, a bird can run rings around an aircraft. The stall-turn is a sharp 180 degrees turn in the air to head in the opposite direction the bird was flying before. It is perhaps the most difficult of the aerobatic manoeuvres. Timing is much more critical in a stall-turn than in any other aerobatic manoeuvre. Using the stall-turn, a bird can cut off an enemy that is pursuing him. The spin is a fast roll in the air that turns a bird into a bullet that defies gravity. A bird in flight in the air spins round in one spot like a rolling dice before flying on. These aerobatic sequences with various variances in between constitute the science and art of aerobatics that each bird must develop and become an expert of.'

Like the Lone Piper had hoped, most of the birds on understanding the theory of aerobatics, the art did not take them long to learn and master. Within the space of five months, most birds had learned the art to a level even the Lone Piper with his robust expectations thought impossible.

'In no distant time, we will all be suicide bombers,' said the Lone Piper. 'We have no choice. We would be killed by toxic substances if we do not kill ourselves and others as suicide bombers. It is better to die with dignity as a suicide bomber than disgracefully without your beak. But for us to be successful suicide bombers, we must develop our flying skills beyond what they are now. We must be able to fly at the altitude of aircrafts and be able to match their speed or even outspeed them.'

The air of excitement that pervaded *the tree of decision* when the Lone Piper began speaking was now being replaced by the air of despondency as the near impossibility of outflying or outspeeding an aircraft possessed the birds. Ruddycheeks articulated the feelings of dejection that had set in by asking, 'how can a bird outspeed an aircraft?'

'Any feat is attainable and in almost anything if there is a *will* to achieve it,' said the Lone Piper. 'Where there is a *will*, there will always be a *way*. Human beings that climbed the alps first set their *will* on the tip of the alps before their bodies were moved to the tip. The *will*, in fact, is a *way* in itself. Like smoke, the *will* rises above all obstacles. *Will* works miracles birds think were worked by supernatural powers when in fact it is the *will* of birds that worked the miracle. Men are able to fly; is it not because of a *will* in them to fly? That men can fly by whatever means, means birds which were created to fly, who indeed men had to build their aircrafts to look like before they can fly, can surely outfly their aircraft imitations. Before now, which bird had thought we can develop the art of aerobatics to the level we have developed it?'

Most birds still looked at the Lone Piper with doubts in their eyes. A plane flies at a supersonic speed; how could a bird surpass it in speed to combat it? How could a bird even match the speed of an aircraft?

'Brassfeathers,' said the Lone Piper, apprehending their thoughts. 'Success is in thoughts, and so is failure. The *will* is a spirit and it travels at the speed of light. You have the choice to release it to bring down a plane or to chain it to doubts of your abilities and die without your beak or without a feather, for we do not know which sickness they would bring to us tomorrow.'

'But I understand a plane has an airborne radar which it uses to see objects eight kilometres away from it; how do we even get close enough to a plane to battle it to the ground when it can see us eight kilometres away and evade us?' asked a bird.

'Unbad thinking, brassfeathers,' said the Lone Piper, looking excited. 'By your thinking, I can see you are already giving *will* a chance and *possibility* a hope. Yes, there is an airborne radar that guides a plane away from obstacles on its path of flight. Luckily for us, birds are usually not considered obstacles to be respected by an aircraft. We are generally not among aviation hazards pilots are weary of and tried to avoid during flights. As far as the pilot is concerned, he has more to fear from the mass of air he flies through than from birds. Birds fear for their own lives and are on the run when they see his plane coming. So he needs not bother about them. That is the contempt in which they hold us. We are something less than dogs to them. This contempt for birds makes it easy for birds to attack an aeroplane. The psychology of a pilot, which holds birds in contempt is a thick cloud mass in the pilot's head that we can hide behind to attack his plane. No airborne radar can see through this cloud. Hiding in this cloud, you don't have to outfly any plane. All you need do is to wait for a plane to fly by you and you attack.'

There was another round of approbation of the Piper's speech.

'But assuming a plane would see a bird and divert, we would hide behind cloud masses in the sky from which we can launch surprise attacks,' continued the Piper. 'You know that is what human hunters do when they attack animals and birds. Hiding behind a cloud, you don't have to outfly any plane. All you need do is to wait for a plane to fly by you and you launch the type of attack you wish.'

From the shrieks, chirping and cooing that followed this speech of the Lone Piper, it was clear the birds were more delighted by it. Faces were now looking more radiant and voices were sounding more resonant.

'What if there are no cloud masses we can hide behind?' asked a bird when the excitement generated by the Piper's speech had died down.

'Outflying aircrafts remains our major assignment,' said the Lone Piper with passion. 'If we can outfly aircrafts, we need no cloud masses to hide and no aircraft using its airborne radar can avoid us. We must therefore have the will and develop the power of outflying aircrafts.'

'How can we achieve such a feat?' a bird wondered aloud.

'Yet, we can,' said another bird. 'Whatever idea the mind can come up with, the mind can come up with the *will* to realize it.'

'*Ideas, will!*' cried Longneck, looking excited. '*Ideas, will,* are the pulleys by which the world is pushed. There is nothing near the greatness of *ideas* and *will* in this world. Birds perished for lack of *ideas* and *will*. Even the food that tends to occupy our minds all the time, great ideas in our heads will place more food in our gizzards.'

'*Will,*' cried Bignose, 'there is nothing that overcomes obstacles like *will*. There is nothing that sustains obstacles like lack of *will*. Even in this debate, it is the *will* of the *Heart of the birds* that kept him above our doubts and fears. Without it, he would have been submerged and drowned in our sea of doubts and fears.'

'Salvation comes only from *ideas* and *will* and this are in the head. Unbad ideas bring salvation. Ungood ideas bring damnation. So each bird carries salvation or damnation in his head,' said Longneck.

'It is incredible to know that a bird can have brilliant ideas like those the *Heart of the birds* has being spinning out,' said Horsevoice. 'Life can only be lived better on new and refreshing perspectives of it. Already I am feeling renewed inside me.'

'And I am feeling fresh outside me,' said Beakybeaky.

'Adversity can be good. Who would have imagined in the good old days that birds can think like this?' said Bignose.

'If we had being thinking like this, human beings would not have even found us in the sky of the earth when they began flying,' said Beakybeaky. 'We would have been flying in the sky of another planet.'

'The idea of birds of the air and lilies of the fields feeding and looking well clothed without having to work for their food or raiment has helped neither the birds of the air nor the lilies of the fields,' said Horsevoice, humorously.

Happy with the new spirit and fervour amongst the birds, the Lone Piper anxious to avoid any view cropping up to introduce fear and doubt again in the birds, decided to railroad them immediately into the cultivation of skills critical to the prosecution of the coming campaign. 'Brassfeathers!' he said, looking at his fellow birds with a warmth and tenderness that a sense of victory had bred, 'we will all move straight to the first phase of exercises that will lead us to the ventilation of our grievances. The first phase is the development of flying skills and power we never know we can have. On top of this tree, *will* yourself that you will shoot into the air with the velocity of a bullet from a gun and *will* yourself to keep moving at that speed for two minutes before stall-turning towards the earth to land on the ground. Mark my words – land on the ground. No bird should land on a tree or any other projectile. You are bound to be dizzy after such a blasting flight. If you land on a projectile, dizziness may toss you to the ground, breaking your neck. But if you land on the ground, you can lie back on your back and suck air into your laboured lungs.'

'Harrrr, kurrr,' the birds chirped to convey understanding.

'You can begin flexing your legs, flapping your wings and stretching your necks before collecting your body into a ramrod like this,' the Lone Piper said, demonstrating to the birds every instructed action.

The birds did as they were instructed.

Poised for flight, the Lone Piper whistled and there was a staccato flurry as all the birds shot into the air with a shocking and frightening speed. The birds sailed up, up, up into the air for a distance about a kilometre before skewing off to head to the ground. It was a breathtaking sight. On the ground, every bird was sprawled on his back heaving and panting, fighting to get back his breath.

'I can even suck in an aeroplane, panting the way I am,' said the Lone Piper when he was beginning to breathe normally again. 'Yes, I can.'

'Which is to say birds in your line of suction had better watch it,' said Longneck, jocularly.

'No, no, no; birds have nothing to fear from my suction,' said the Lone Piper with a mischievous gleam on his face. It's lousy human beings and their lousy aircrafts that have to watch it.'

'What a fantastic possibility!' exclaimed Ruddycheeks. 'Birds sucking in aircrafts!'

'That would be a very fair outcome,' said Longneck. 'After feeding on us, it would be meet for us to feed on aircrafts.'

'We can all go and find food now,' said the Lone Piper, getting up from where he had been lying on his back taking lungful breaths. 'After we have rested, in the evening, I, Longneck, Beakybeaky, Horsevoice, Bignose and some *minta* birds would fly to the nearby Bozuwa airport to reconnoitre it, and if circumstances allow, plant poison in an aircraft. Until we feel we are ready to start a war with aircrafts in the air, aerobatic exercises, reconnoitring of airports and planting of poison in the engines of aircrafts would be part of our daily routines. From now on, let the gentiles look not to uzza the cave of refuge, for their end has come.'

Giddy with happiness, all the birds flew away to find food for the day.

Chapter Eight

Bozuwa airport was an international airport from which an average of ten flights took off every day. All year round, but more in the dry season than the rainy season, the grass strip beyond the tarmac was always full of grasshoppers. When a plane was taking off or landing, the wind from the engines of the plane rustled the grasses near the runway and the grasshoppers perched on the grasses leapt into the air in fright before settling down again on the grass strip to continue foraging for the food that kept them there. Sometimes grasshoppers that leapt into the air upon a plane landing or taking off do not make it back to the grass again but to the gizzards of birds that frequent the airport looking for food. Different species of birds came to the airport to feed on the grasshoppers. Whenever a plane was landing or taking off and grasshoppers jumped into the air in fright, they were snapped up by the birds. Not only birds, even cows sometimes strayed into the airport to graze on the lush grasses of the airport particularly in the rainy season. About two years ago, there was a report of a near fatal collision between a landing aircraft and cows grazing in the airport.

Because the airport was a sort of melting pot for grasshoppers, birds and even cows, the presence of birds in the airport excited no interest. So, when the Lone Piper and his companions arrived the airport on their reconnoitre mission, no one paid them attention. They landed in the airport towards sunset.

By then the airport had already closed to air traffic; so, there were few people around. There was only one airport security man pacing up and down the frontage of the passengers' waiting room. He did not even see the birds landing in the airport. From the expression on his face, he seemed to be worried by something outside his job, which he would rather were solved than he attending to his duty.

Unseen by the security man, the Lone Piper and his companions moved towards the plane nearest to them and entered the two engines of the aircraft, which were both uncovered. The Lone Piper standing by the air-intake directed a *minta* bird to walk past the guide-veins and deposit his excreta inside the engine. In the other engine, the other birds were doing the same thing. In a moment, the mission that brought the birds to the airport was accomplished and they flew back to Kirkina savannah without the security man even knowing they had visited the airport.

Back in the savannah, the birds were in an ecstatic mood. Their first outing in the prosecution of their campaign against aircrafts and those who fly them had been extraordinarily easy and successful. Birds that were not part of the reconnoitre mission gathered round the Lone Piper and his companions to know how the mission fared.

'Wonderfully swell!' exclaimed the Lone Piper in an upbeat mood. 'Nothing can be easier or more successful. It seems all the gods of the world are in support of our campaign.'

'Why should they not be when human beings have ganged up to wipe birds out of the surface of the earth?' interjected a bird.

'Like I was saying,' continued the Lone Piper, 'we got to the airport to meet a security man more absorbed by his own problems than watching over the airport which he is paid to do.'

'Because they sow misery for other creatures, human beings will always be miserable,' interjected Ruddycheeks. 'You cannot sow misery for others and reap happiness for yourself.'

'Will you allow the *Heart of the birds* to tell us how the mission went or you will keep interrupting him?' a bird eager to know what actually happened at the airport said, exasperated by the frequent interruption of the Lone Piper.

'Some birds are beginning to behave like human beings; their mouths are always itching to talk,' said another bird also eager to know what happened at the airport. 'Very soon, some of us will need the ring in the pig's snout. *Heart of the birds*, please tell us what happened at the airport.'

'The security man on duty like I said was too preoccupied with his worries to see or take any interest in us. So, we walked casually to a plane and flew into its engines unseen by the security man who was no more guarding the airport than the grass in the airport were. A *minta* bird and I entered one engine of the plane while Longneck and another *minta* bird entered the other engine. I remained by the air-intake of the engine while the *minta* bird went beyond the guide veins to deposit his poison in the belly of the engine, the way they had been depositing human flu in the belly of our savannah. Longneck and the other *minta* bird did the same thing to the other engine and off we flew away unseen as we flew in.

'You are making it sound as easy as perching on a tree branch and farting,' said one of the birds after the Lone Piper had finished telling them how he and the other birds prosecuted their assignment.

'It was about that easy,' said Beakybeaky. 'But it was more exciting than farting on a tree branch because in this case the tree branch we were farting on will later kill our enemy.'

The Lone Piper who since he played his pipe on *the mountain of blood* after the bloodbath had not played it again to a large and close audience began to play his pipe.

> Meat was shared equally
> Between the hyena and the leopard
> But since the hyena is a glutton
> He must eat his share and that of the
leopard
> And that was why he fell into the hole
> The leopard dug for him.
> Konso, I asked you to lend me love
> But you lent me hate
> I ask you to lend me life
> But you lent me death
> Now is the time for payment of debts
> And you are demanding
> That I pay you love

When it was hate you lent me
That I pay you life
When it was death you lent me
Someone should tell Konso
To stop being funny
Someone should tell Konso
That I invested the hate he lent me
And it has yielded a lot of interest
Someone should tell Konso
That I will pay him back his hate with
interest

Someone should tell Konso
That I invested death that he lent me
And it has yielded a lot of interest
Someone should tell Konso
That I will pay him back his death with
interest

When the Lone Piper finished playing, there was
a new fruiting and seasoning of life. Birds of fire,
birds of ashes, birds of water and lightning moved
about him in the spirit world.

Chapter Nine

A day after the Lone Piper and his companions returned from the airport, two black-crested birds – Wildclaws and Darkhead, were on a tree not far away from *the mountain of blood* chatting, not knowing there was a fire-crested bird – Blueeyes on the same tree.

'Fire-crested birds are barbarians,' said Wildclaws, 'and barbaric birds will always be governed by cultured birds. That is why it is a black-crested bird that is the *Heart* and saviour of all birds today.'

Blueeyes the fire-crested bird on the tree was shocked to hear this severe disparagement of his tribe coming from a black-crested bird. Was it the view of this black-crested bird alone or the view of all black-crested birds? he wondered, anger gripping him.

'You know when we talk of humans as gentiles, I think the true gentiles are fire-crested birds; they are the real barbarians who had no leader until they met us,' said Darkhead, the other black-crested bird. 'Each of them trusted only to the wealth his beak could peck to his nest without thought of the commonwealth of security that a leader provides. But when we made them see the benefits of leadership, you saw how quickly they submitted to our leadership.'

'We black-crested birds are destined to rule the world; yes, it is our destiny to rule the world and I am happy to see we are beginning to take this divine responsibility seriously,' said Wildclaws. 'From the beginning of the world, it was destined that the saviour of all birds on earth would be a black-crested bird and I am happy that while I am still alive, the messiah came.'

'But why should the messiah of birds be a black-crested bird?' asked Blueeyes, the fire-crested bird on the tree with the two black crested birds. He was unable to contain any longer his rising anger at what the two black-crested birds were saying.

The black-crested birds were startled to know they were not alone on the tree. A fire-crested bird was with them and all they had said against fire-crested birds had fallen into his ears. They felt foolish for not having taken care to ascertain there was no other bird on the tree before they started shooting off their mouths. Well, it was out. They must find a way of hushing it so that it does not get to the ears of other fire-crested birds or for that matter, the ears of the Lone Piper.

'We have no coal here,' the two black-crested birds heard Blueeyes the fire-crested bird saying. 'How do we even come by black-crested birds?' What we have here is the sun and fire-crested birds are children of the sun which gave them their fiery crests.'

'We did not mean what we were saying,' said Wildclaws. 'We were only having one of those humours birds have now and then.'

'From jokes to jabs is the rattle of life,' said Blueeyes. 'A joke always denigrates a bird. If the denigrated bird takes offence at his denigration, he jabs at the bird that denigrated him. If he does not jab at the bird laughing at his expense, the laughing bird is encouraged by his inert sense of insult to jab at him. In this case, we fire-crested birds were the ones that insulted ourselves by accepting a black-crested bird as our *Heart*. This makes it so easy for you to jab at us. If we laugh this off as a joke when in fact it is a jab, you will kick us as men kick their dogs.'

'Believe us, we were only joking,' said Wildclaws alarmed by the bitterness of Blueeyes.

'For you to insult fire-crested birds and tell me you were joking shows your low opinion of the intelligence of fire-crested birds,' said Blueeyes whose anger instead of shrinking seemed to be ballooning. 'You were having a humour and you were saying such wicked things against my tribe? You were so earnest in your ridicule of my tribe and yet you meant your jibes to be humour. I looked at the faces of both of you and I did not see any humour there. Rather what I saw was arrogance and scorn for my tribe.'

We would only make matters worse if we try to fob him off thought Darkhead. The best thing is to apologise. As Darkhead was thinking of apology, Wildclaws was not thinking of any such thing; rather he was thinking of killing Blueeyes and burying the matter on the tree they were.

'We are sorry for saying such unseemly things about your tribe,' said Darkhead, fervently. 'To err is birdlike and to forgive is also birdlike. Please, forgive us and let this matter not go beyond this tree. Let it be a little secret between three-bird brothers.'

Blueeyes shook his head.

'We fought an ethnic war not long ago in this savannah, we may not survive one more so soon after,' said Darkhead, looking pleadingly at Blueeyes.

'You should have thought of that before spiting on our faces,' said Blueeyes. 'We saw you and greeted you. But, instead of returning our greeting, you are throwing insults at us and you expect us to continue greeting you. Chirr,' hissed Blueeyes.

Wildclaws hopped twice towards the fire-crested bird. He knows he alone could not kill Blueeyes. But he was sure Darkhead would not just look on without giving a helping hand. How could Darkhead ever think he could apologise to a barbarian? Apology is only for the civil. The barbarian who attacks without being attacked cannot be appeased by apology. The only thing that would appease his thirst for blood is to hit back; not once, but twice.

'We are no more brothers than the snake and the frog are,' Wildclaws heard Blueeyes saying as he hopped the third time towards the aggrieved bird. 'The monkey and the chimpanzee may have one or two things in common, but the monkey is a monkey and the chimpanzee is a chimpanzee. I wonder how we fire-crested birds came to accept a black-crested bird as our *Heart* in the first place. It is unbad that you have shown our stupidity to us so soon.'

By the time Blueeyes finished talking, Wildclaws who had been hopping towards him was almost within a striking distance of him. Darkhead watching

Wildclaws knew what he wanted to do, but somehow did not feel unduly alarmed, terrible as he thought what Wildclaws wanted to do was. Wildclaws was his friend and he knew how coldblooded he could be. One day, they had gone to drink water in the river where they met a finch who had also come to the river to drink. When the finch finished drinking the water, he flew up a tree branch where he was chirping noisily and looking down on the two black-crested birds still inside the river drinking. In the river, Wildclaws was seething with anger. While drinking the water, the finch who was upstream had muddied the water, which had flowed towards the two black-crested birds drinking downstream. When the finch finished drinking, he flew up a high branch of a tree on the riverbank without any word of farewell to the two black-crested birds. On the tree branch, the finch began to chirp noisily exasperating them with his noise. Wildclaws had sworn to deal with the finch. Two days later, he went to the nest of the finch at night and murdered him in his sleep. So the moment Wildclaws began hopping towards Blueeyes, Darkhead knew he wanted to kill him. Watching Blueeyes talked, Darkhead could not know whether the arrowed bird was sensing the danger creeping towards him or not.

As Wildclaws was about taking the last hop that would bring him on top of Blueeyes, the later flew several paces away.

'In addition to denigrating us,' you want to kill us!' cried Blueeyes where he was now perching; 'and you call yourselves a civilized race?'

What you are saying shows how ignorant you are, thought Wildclaws. For others to accept you as their superior in civilization tomorrow, you have to overwhelm them with primitive behaviour today. In an air-to-air combat, he and Darkhead could kill Blueeyes. But that would be an open fight that would attract other birds. No, Blueeyes must be killed on the tree before he spills the beans to his fellows.

'Talk not of killing,' said Darkhead. 'We have seen too many deaths in this savannah in recent times for us to want to see more. Even if we are vampires, we should be sick of the taste of blood on our tongues by now.'

Darkhead was still talking when Wildclaws leapt for Blueeyes, murder on his beak and claws. Blueeyes flew away pursued by the two desperate black-crested birds.

Chapter Ten

Twice, Wildclaws pursuing Blueeyes pecked the latter's tail, pulling off a wad of plumage. Each time Blueeyes was pecked, he screamed in pain and anger. But knowing Darkhead was also pursuing him, he could not turn round to engage Wildclaws in a fight. Like a little flame that fuel and air were running out on, Blueeyes was flaring out. However, if fuel and air were running out of the flame in flight, the flames in pursuit seemed to be taking over the fuel and air the fleeing flame was losing. In a burst of new energy, Wildclaws overtook Blueeyes and headed him off the path he was fleeing which was taking them to a string of trees most of the fire-crested birds lived. Blueeyes was now between the two black-crested birds. This increased his fright, tipping him to panic.

Fire-crested birds on trees and in the grass of the savannah on hearing and seeing a fellow fire-crested bird screaming between two black-crested birds pecking him, flew into the air to help. In the air, the fire-crested birds who had gone to help their kind, engaged the black-crested birds in a fierce battle. Black-crested birds in the grass and on trees seeing many fire-crested birds pecking two black-crested birds also joined the aerial combat. Feathers started dropping to the ground in plums. Soon two black-crested birds and a fire-crested bird fell to the ground, dead.

The Lone Piper who was having a nap in his nest was woken up by the great commotion in the air.

What he saw filled him with shock and awe. Fire-crested birds and black-crested birds were pecking ferociously at each other and flinging uprooted plumage around with sickening relish. By a common reflex, he began piping:

Songs of the waking day, wings of the setting sun
Flapping out life what will you breathe tomorrow?
Flapping out unity which bird can fly with one wing?
When we use our beaks to peck at ourselves
We will have no beaks to peck at the enemy
Which snake ever turns its poison upon itself?
The warmth of the air and the joy of the lonely stars
Are commonwealths we both enjoy
We all live on trees and carry feathers on our backs
Kill not the one that shares poison with you in the air
The bird that does so shorten his life
Because he will now have to take all the poison alone
Instead of turning our frustrations upon ourselves
We should empty them on those spreading poison for us in the air

Friends are eating friends and the enemy is happy

Brothers are at war over their mother's nest

And their evil uncle would grab the nest

Give peace and happiness to your brother

And he will give you a wing to fight your enemy

You are sowing death for fellow birds

And *the clutches-dependent cripple* will harvest life.

The birds upon hearing this song stopped fighting and lighted either on a tree or on the ground. The riotous savannah was now quiet and serene again. But in the new serenity of the savannah, the fetid odour of an uprising that just subsided was sensible.

'Fire-crested birds and black-crested birds!' cried the Lone Piper. 'Why are you fighting and killing yourselves again. What happened?'

Blueeyes that knew what happened was fatally wounded in the fight and could not talk. Wildclaws and Darkhead who knew the cause of the fracas would also not talk. The rest of the birds, who joined the fight in defence of their kind not knowing the cause of the fight, could also not talk.

'Why are you all quiet? Is there no bird that can tell me why we are fighting and killing ourselves so soon after the bloodbath on *the mountain of blood*?'

asked the Lone Piper, looking about him for a bird that would speak.

'To say the truth,' said a fire-crested bird to the right of the Lone Piper, 'Only Blueeyes, Wildclaws and Darkhead know the cause of this fight and can tell us. We were rooting for food under a demba tree when we saw Blueeyes being attacked in midair by Wildclaws and Darkhead. We flew into the air to defend Blueeyes. Black-crested birds also flew into the air to defend their own. That was how the whole thing started.'

'You mean no bird tried to find out the cause of the fight between the three birds before all of you started fighting each other?' asked the Lone Piper, shocked by what he was hearing.

'As far as I know, no bird did,' said the same fire-crested bird.

For a while the Lone Piper did not say anything. He was thinking. Since Wildclaws and Darkhead were before him and had chosen to be quiet on the cause of the fight, it meant they were at fault and could not be relied on for the truth. If he must know the true cause of the fracas, he must rely on Blueeyes lying on the ground fatally wounded. He went to the injured bird and tried to find out from him why he and the two black-crested birds were fighting.

Gasping and stuttering, Blueeyes told the Lone Piper how he eavesdropped on Wildclaws and Darkhead denigrating fire-crested birds, which led to their chasing him to kill him to hush up the matter.

Other birds were also by Blueeyes while he was telling the Lone Piper the cause of the fracas; but no bird heard nor understood all the dying bird was saying. Only the Lone Piper who had his right ear by the mouth of the dying bird did. When Blueeyes finished talking, the Lone Piper stood up and told the birds what the dying bird told him. When he finished reporting to the assembly of birds what the dying bird told him, there was an uproar of anger and protest from the fire-crested birds.

'Am I unright in being transparent?' asked the Lone Piper.

In place of the loud protest by the fire-crested birds, there were now murmurings and low hisses. They were divided. A few fire-crested birds were of the view they should denounce the Lone Piper as their *Heart*, while the majority preferred to still have him as their *Heart*. According to the majority, it was not the Lone Piper that made Wildclaws and Darkhead to say the reported hateful things. In fact, the Lone Piper had always shown deference to them by calling their name first before calling the name of black-crested birds in all his speeches. They must not allow their grief over the uncouth utterances of only two black-crested birds blind them to the good qualities of the Piper.

'Perhaps, you would have preferred I play politics with the matter,' said the Lone Piper But as you know, I am not a politician and therefore cannot play politics. 'Wildclaws and Darkhead, come out here and look me in the eye and tell me what Blueeyes told me was not true,' he called the two birds, beckoning at them simultaneously.

The two birds went and stood before the Lone Piper and the assembly of birds, but could not look at the Lone Piper or say anything.

'So Blueeyes was telling the truth?' said the Lone Piper half question, half statement.

The two birds still did not say anything.

'It is unfortunate that you chose to cause division among us at a time we need all the unity we can get to fight a common enemy threatening us with misery and death. For causing this unnecessary acrimony and deaths, you have shown yourselves to be ungood birds. For sowing unlove among birds which has led to *ourcide*, you are banished from this savannah and you are condemned to die by ghosts-strike wherever you flee to.'

The two black-crested birds started shrieking wildly saying the punishment was excessive while other birds, particularly fire-crested birds, were chirping to each other in jubilation.

After this, the birds dispersed.

In a secret meeting of only black-crested birds called by the Lone Piper the night of that day, the Piper warned them to be more discreet with their tongues. 'I am the *Heart* of this savannah. Without being told, you should know any act of arrogance by you, would be seen by other birds as you telling them you are superior birds because it is one of you that is *Heart*. If you go beyond arrogance to outright insults like Wildclaws and Darkhead did today, you know what to expect. I am still rather surprised we did not get a worse reaction than what we got.'

'Perhaps because the fire-crested birds knew Wildclaws and Darkhead were speaking the truth,' said a bird.

'Ssh…'

'I don't think *Heart of the birds* you are right to seek to speak the truth the way you spoke it today,' said Beakybeaky. 'Like it or not, you are a politician and as a politician, you should not ask for courage to speak the truth, but wisdom to say what people will be happy to hear whether it is the truth or a lie. That is the only way you will endure on your throne. A politician is not a witness in court required to say the whole truth and nothing but the truth, but a charmer required to say what will please the birds. It matters little if what he said will later kill the birds. Law and politics do not always meet. To succeed as a politician, what you need is guile not honesty. A bird that will succeed as a Casanova can easily succeed as a politician because smooth talk is required for both arts.'

'Beakybeaky, I agree with you,' said another bird. 'Politics is different from law. While the law asks for the whole truth, politics ask for the whole lie, half-truth or quarter truth.'

'Who told you I told the whole truth today?' asked the Lone Piper with twinkles of mischief in his eyes which the birds could not see in the darkness of the night.

Every bird looked at him in surprise.

'Blueeyes told me our brothers said fire-crested birds are barbarians that ought to be happy they are governed by black-crested birds; but you know I did not say such a thing to the assembly of birds,' said the Lone Piper.

The other birds were now looking at the Lone Piper with astonishment on their faces.

'The sentences you passed on Wildclaws and Darkhead were excessive,' said a bird, trying to take advantage of the new soft Lone Piper he saw.

'It is politically correct to punish your own excessively where he has been excessive with his mouth,' said the Lone Piper in a stern voice. After saying this, he flew away to his nest and the meeting disbanded.

'A politician is a funny bird,' said Beakybeaky, after the Lone Piper had left. 'A politician is both a snake and a bird-poacher. As a snake, he is slippery and dangerous. As a bird-poacher, he goes out to ensnare trusting birds totally shorn of tricks. Knowing himself to be a snake, he sees every bird as a snake that he must charm else it will do mischief on election day. So in addition to being a bird poacher, he is also a snake charmer.'

'You can go on and on saying politicians are snakes till the end of your days and no one will disagree with you,' said Bignose. 'Who would have thought the *Heart of the birds* was telling us half-truths and polished lies? Who knows if it was even the *Heart of the birds* that finished off Blueeyes to hush up the truth. A politician is not a snake for nothing. His poison is always there to serve him.'

'No, Bignose,' said Beakybeaky. 'Your big nose is smelling something where there is nothing. Blueeyes died from the mortal wounds he received in the fight not from the *Heart of the birds'* sleight of hand. Yes, the *Heart of the birds* is a politician; but that does not make him the devil.'

'Beakybeaky, for the second time today you have said what my ears want to hear,' said a bird. 'To me, a politician is both God and the devil. Often when he speaks to me, I don't know who of the two is speaking.'

'Kirrr, sirrrr' the birds laughed and flew to their nests for the night.

Chapter Eleven

It was from Longneck that other birds of Kirkina savannah first heard of the crash of the aircraft the *minta* birds first excreted inside its engines. Longneck as one of the birds that went with the *minta* birds that excreted inside the engines of the plane, knew the plane very well. He was a keen observer of minute details of situations and anything he came into contact with. Nothing escaped his pecking eyes. Like a powerful magnet picks all metals it is passed over, his eyes picked into the inner recess of his mind, minute features of things they were passed over. When the *minta* birds had excreted inside the engines of the aircraft, he had taken in the aircraft's general colour, the stripes on its wings and tail and a grey patch on its nozzle. When he went grazing in Huahua jungle and saw the wreckage of a crashed aircraft, he went to inspect it and immediately recognised the wreckage as the aircraft *minta* birds excreted inside its engines. He was ecstatic. Their campaign against aircrafts was getting off to a successful start. He immediately flew back to Kirkina savannah to inform the Lone Piper and other birds of his finding.

News of the crash of the aircraft was received in Kirkina savannah first with disappointment and later with happiness. Where were they in the sky when the plane dropped out of the sky? Where were the children of the sky when the intruder got a kick from the sky? They should have been there to watch the joyful mishap taking place. Gradually, however, disappointed was replaced with euphoria that built into a jamboree later in the evening. Immediately the birds were informed of the crash by Longneck, they set out to Huahua jungle to see things for themselves. When the Lone Piper and the other birds that sowed the seed of its destruction saw the wreckage of the crashed aircraft, they also recognised it as the aircraft the *minta* birds excreted in its engines in Bozuwa airport. For a long while, they hopped about ecstatically on the ruins of the crashed aircraft. The crashed aircraft created a wreckage trail of about 1240 metres that was mostly burned parts of the destroyed aircraft. The aircraft while still in the air must have caught fire and disintegrated before crashing into the forest, the birds thought.

From what the birds could see, it was not long the air mishap happened. Ashes of burned parts of the aircraft still looked fresh and not much dust had collected on the carcass of the aircraft. Smears of blood of victims of the crash could still be seen on some fragments of the crashed aircraft. What looked like a burnt, decapitated human hand was found near the head of the aircraft. It was so thrilling to the birds beholding these grisly images of the crash.

'This blood will atone for the blood of Flaming Eyes that was shed on *the mountain of blood*,' said the Lone Piper, sticking one of his claws into a dry, patch of blood under a piece of wreckage.

'This hand pulled out of a man and burned to this charred horror is atonement for my friend

Bubbleheart who died of the horrible disease,' said a bird.

'This is their own *mountain of blood*,' said the Lone Piper, excitedly. 'You cannot kill us and make us kill ourselves and expect that we will go into a Biantu and be crying like Kujen, without hitting back at you.'

'Even Kujen who went into a Biantu and wept for three years for his dead mother did so out of a contrite spirit of having in a way caused his mother's death,' said Bignose. 'Yes, we might have caused our brothers' deaths, but it was your treachery that made us to do it. Yes, we might have killed some of our number when differences arose between Blueeyes, Wildclaws and Darkhead, but your treachery caused the differences the three brothers had.'

'Instead of going into a Biantu, we would go into the engines of your aircrafts and turn them from the flying coffins they have always been into graves in the air,' said another bird.

'The taste of your enemy's blood is never bland. Instead, it has such a delicate taste,' said Ruddycheeks.

'There is a singular way in which what has happened excites me,' said the Lone Piper, a bemused expression on his face. 'They flew over our savannah and dropped poison without us knowing. We started dying without knowing what was killing us until Flaming Eyes discovered the cause of our deaths. Without them knowing, we went and planted poison in the engines of their plane – it may even be the same plane that dropped the poison in our savannah. Without knowing they were flying with poison in the heart of the plane, they roamed the skies without a thought of danger until the plane crashed waking them up to death. Even when it crashed, they would not know what caused the engine to fail, until perhaps the black box tells them.' Mentioning the black box, the heart of the Lone Piper began to beat faster. Immediately he saw how good it would have been for them to have been the ones that retrieved the black box and the cockpit voice recorder from the wreckage of the crashed aircraft before human beings did so. Without the black box and the cockpit voice recorder, the cause of the engine failure would remain a mystery. But with the flight recorders, the cause of the crash could easily be determined. A decoding of the recorders would reveal the engines quitted and failed because birds excreted inside them. This will make the aviation industry cover the mouths of their engines to make access into the engines by birds impossible.

'It is unfortunate we did not arrive at the scene of this crash early enough,' he said with a bitter note in his voice. If we had, we would have recovered the black box and the cockpit voice recorder from the wreckage of the crash before they did so.'

'What is a black box and cockpit voice recorder?' asked Beakybeaky.

The black box and the cockpit voice recorder are flight recorders in an aircraft that record details of the aircraft's flight performance. The details recorded can be used to discover the cause of a crash.'

'But as you can see *Heart of the birds*, almost everything in this aircraft was burned,' a bird said. 'So, the black box and cockpit recorder must have been burnt with every other thing.'

'The black box and the cockpit voice recorder are made with platinum,' said the Lone Piper. 'They are fire and water resistant. No fire can melt them and no water can destroy them. They are built to survive an air-crash and tell the story of the crash.'

'These human beings,' grumbled Bignose. 'Their efforts to secure themselves know no limits.'

'Fingerprints left behind by criminals, especially murderers, are critical in hunting down the criminals,' said Longneck who like the Lone Piper knew much about the black box and the cockpit recorder. In a case like ours, the black box and the cockpit reorder would be like fingerprints we left behind in the aircraft engines when we went to excrete in them. They may not be used to trace us, but they can be used to determine with precision the cause of the engines' failure.'

'Human beings are smart,' said a bird. 'We have to hand it to them. Even if you don't like a horse, you must agree it is a beautiful creature. Seeing they are not likely to survive an air-crash, they made recorders to survive the crash and tell the story of how the crash happened. This is the mind of a beast that wants to speak from the grave.'

'Longneck, since you know how important the black box and the cockpit voice recorder are, they should have been the first things you looked for when you saw the crash before running to the savannah to tell us,' a bird said.

'In the excitement I found myself, I never thought anything about the flight recorders,' said Longneck. 'But there is no much time lag between the time I discovered the crash and now. If the flight recorders were here when I first saw the crash, they are likely to still be here.'

'You are right there,' said the Lone Piper with amiability on his face that a new thought had kindled. 'What Longneck just said has reminded me that there are times when the flight recorders are not found immediately after the crash. Where they fall clear of the crashed plane and under a forest growth, finding them may not be easy. Even where they are part of the wreckage, finding them in the midst of the wreckage may still be difficult. At any rate, after a crash, the minds of people were always more on rescuing any survivor of the crash than finding the flight recorders. This mindset sometimes delays the finding of the recorders. So it is possible that the flight recorders might still be somewhere in this forest if they are not in the wreckage. So, it may not be a bad idea if we search the wreckage and the forest for them.

'But even if we find the flight recorders, they may be too heavy for us to carry,' said a bird.

'You have said something,' said the Lone Piper. 'But I believe with *will* we can carry any of these recorders. If an eagle cannot carry them, we will destroy them with our, excreta, beaks and talons.'

'What a crash could not destroy how do you destroy it with your beak and talon?'

'What cannot be destroyed by fire and water, how do beaks and talons destroy it?'

'The desert may not be able to kill the camel, but a small thing like the scorpion kills it,' said the Lone Piper. 'If our excreta can corrode the engine of an aircraft and make it pack up, our excreta or beaks and talons can destroy the black box and the cockpit voice recorder.'

There were loud shrieks of approval of what the Lone Piper had said.

It was agreed it would be a good thing for them to ferret around for the flight recorders given their importance. Immediately they began to look for the recorders in the wreckage of the aircraft. But the problem was that only the Lone Piper and Longneck knew what the flight recorders look like. So other birds kept calling them to come and see if what they had found was one of the flight recorders. This turned out to be very torturous to the Lone Piper and Longneck. Each time they rushed to answer a call hoping one of the recorders had been found only to find it was either a piece of burned metal of the crashed aircraft or an item from a passenger's luggage. The Lone Piper and Longneck had to explain to the other birds what the recorders look like to reduce the frequency they were called to see if a turned-up object was one of the recorders. Birds crept under broken sheets, peeped into crevices of the wreckage and pecked to turn over what they thought was one of the recorders, but none of the recorders was found in the wreckage.

'It is possible they might be somewhere in the forest,' said the Lone Piper keen on finding the flight recorders.

'But we can't search the whole forest?' protested a bird. 'The forest is too vast for us to comb looking for the flight recorders.'

'*Will* brassfeathers,' said the Lone Piper. 'There is no obstacle the *will* cannot overcome. *Will* is to birds what faith is to humans. It can cast away mountains.'

'Except that it cannot produce flight recorders that have already been taken away by those who were here before us,' said a bird.

'It is always like this,' said the Lone Piper. 'Birds without *will* are birds without eyes. Because they stumble and fall over short distances, they tell you your destination is too far. They try to make those with *will* see how impossible it is to achieve a goal. They are like newts. They have eyes, but the eyes are covered with bone or skin. So, their eyes which were supposed to see outside, see only their anuses. They spent their days burrowing into the earth near their anuses because their eyes cannot see the beauty of the sky they would have flown into. That is why they don't amount to anything in life. That is why other amphibians that listen to them never amount to anything in life. Anything that cannot fly cannot amount to anything in life. That is why men invented the aircraft.'

'The forest belongs to us,' said Longneck who like the Piper desperately wanted the flight recorders found. 'The forest is our home. There is no square metre of it that we don't know. There is hardly a tree of it we have not lighted or roosted on. If human beings who are aliens to the forest can search and find something in the forest, we to whom the forest is a home can find it much faster.'

The Lone Piper and Longneck having spoken like this, the other birds agreed that the forest be searched for the flight recorders.

'We don't have to find it today,' said the Lone Piper. 'In fact, it looks like we cannot possibly find it today. We search today the portion of the forest we can. The portion that remains unsearched, we search some other day.'

The other birds nodded their assent and spread into the forest to begin the search. They had not searched far when investigators of the air-crash who had been searching for the flight recorders for more than a week arrived the forest to continue their search.

Chapter Twelve

The aircraft that crashed had QYS11346 call sign. It departed Bozuwa airport at 1226 hrs on a scheduled passenger flight enroute Kouta, with 120 passengers and 7 crewmembers on board.

On-site investigation could not begin immediately because the crash site was remote and difficult to access. For two days, where the aircraft crashed was not even known. It was merely described as *the missing aircraft*. When the crashed site was found by a search team in a helicopter, access to the site was difficult. Hiking through a rugged terrain covered with thick vegetation, rescue teams and investigators were continually bogged-down by a thunderous jungle that had little lightning in it. When they got to the crash site, the remains of a once graceful airliner shattered into a thousand pieces lay strewn over a long wreckage trail. The aircraft had impacted on tall trees that before the crash stood like forest icons licking the sky. Apart from the nozzle, a few pieces of fuselage and the remains of a wing, the only significant remains of the aircraft was the rear empennage consisting of the vertical fin and one horizontal stabilizer. The remaining wreckage resembled shredded pieces of foil sighing in the desolation of the crash.

Meteorological conditions at the time of the crash obtained from a meteorological agency showed the wind was 360/16kts, visibility – 2800m, clouds were not so dense and temperature was 27C.

Though these were not optimum weather conditions for flight, they were not weather conditions that would necessarily lead to a crash. Weather as a factor for the crash having been substantially discounted, attention shifted to human error, machine or instrument failure as possible causes of the crash.

There were allegations and counter allegations of whether man or machine caused the crash. Banjos aeronautics makers of the aircraft and its maintainers maintained that their aircrafts had no history of air-crashes as they were well built with various redundancies to fall back on in the event of a mechanical failure during flight. Aircraft information showed that the aircraft was only six years old. It was maintained in accordance with the prescribed schedule of maintenance and inspections. The aircraft maintainers also claimed that they carried out progressive checks on their aircrafts religiously. It was not known in the history of the company to exceed by an hour the 50 hours, 100 hours or annual checks on their aircrafts. The last cycle checks were carried out at airframe time of 49802.23 hrs at the Air Holland Business Civil Aviation Aircraft (BCAA) approved maintenance organization. The aircraft was up to date in its compliance with service bulletins and airworthiness directives. It had a valid certificate of airworthiness till 17 January. It was certified airworthy to fly on the day of the crash. As far as they were concerned, the crash was not caused by a failure of their machine but by human error.

Homma the owner of the airline maintained that the crash must have been caused by a failure of the aircraft as his personnel had no history of causing air mishaps. The Commander of the aircraft, a 48-year-old man with licence No. ATPL 3029, had aircraft ratings on BACI-11, F-27, MD-80, DC-9 and a total flying experience of 12, 047 hours out of which 1, 800 hours were on type. He had his last stimulator training at PANAM International Flight Academy Miami, USA. Other crewmembers were also well trained, well paid and committed to their job.

Because of this shifting of blame, there was a lot of enthusiasm both by the makers of the aircraft and its owners, but more by its makers, to find the black box and the cockpit voice recorder which would likely show who or what was to blame for the mishap. Usually, finding the two important flight recorders depends on the severity of the crash and the terrain the crash took place. The more severe the crash, the more likely it is that finding the flight recorders would take time. But if it is less severe, the recorders are likely to be found faster. If the crash takes place in a bush, a forest or at sea, finding the recorders is also likely to be more difficult. But if it is in an open land, finding the recorders is likely to be easy. This crash was severe and it took place in a forest with bogs. Sifting through the wreckage of the crash in a bog was a treacherous task. There were monkeys and gorillas in the jungle. There were snakes and hyenas hissing and howling against the invasion of their habitats. A tiger in its patch startled by the intrusion of a searcher leapt at his throat. The jungle was alive with danger and death.

The metal cradles that contained the recorders were found after five days of the search. It looked like the recorders were thrown clear of the main wreckage. The searchers now began to search along the trajectories they thought, from the position of the metal cradles, the flight recorders must have been thrown. However, vigorous and thorough as they searched, they did not find the flight recorders along the trajectories they were searching for them.

But the company that made the aircraft was determined to find the two flight recorders and clear itself of blame if the crash was not caused by the failure of its machines or instruments. If the crash was caused by the failure of its machines or instruments, to improve them. So, it did not give up the search for the recorders. Instead, it brought more searchers to forage and dig around for the flight recorders. For days, the crash site like a witch held to the vital recorders of the crashed aircraft fanning desperation and exasperation in those searching for the flight recorders.

But the searchers would not give up. Most of the wreckage was buried in muddy ground, which they had to dig hoping to turn up the flight recorders. Each evening, they would meet to talk about their experience in the search and to compare results of the day's work.

On the day the birds found the wreckage of the aircraft, searchers of the flight recorders were delayed from coming to search for the recorders by lack of aviation fuel in the helicopter which was to bring them to the crash site.

As the birds searched for the recorders, they heard the sound of a helicopter above their heads. They all lifted their eyes and saw the helicopter alighting some distance away from where they were. The birds did not immediately know what brought the helicopter to the crash site. But as soon as three men alighted from the aircraft and began searching the forest, they suspected they must be searching for the flight recorders, and as it later turned out, they were right in their suspicion. The men were searching for the flight recorders.

The Lone Piper was ecstatic. 'You can see that they have come to look for what we are looking for,' he said to the birds. 'It means the flight recorders have not been found.'

'That is true,' said Longneck. 'We can now search for the recorders knowing they are still in the forest. 'We stand as good a chance as they in finding the recorders.'

'I will say we stand a better chance,' said Beakybeaky. 'They don't know the forest the way we do.'

We should not let them know we are searching for the flight recorders,' said Bignose to Beakybeaky who was ferreting for the recorders near him. 'If they know we are ferreting for the recorders, they will suspect our involvement in the crash.'

'And I have not thought of that before now,' said Beakybeaky. 'I don't think the *Heart of the birds* and Longneck who are so intent on the search have thought of this either. As yet, no one suspects our involvement in causing the crash. But our action can make us suspects.'

'I have thought of that,' said the Lone Piper when Beakybeaky raised the issue with him. 'But human beings are not as intelligent as you think. Even if they see us ferreting this forest with them, they will think nothing of our action beyond the fact that we are ferreting for food. To them we have no intelligence beyond the instinct of scratching the forest for food.'

The three searchers that came to look for the flight recorders were surprised to find so many birds in the forest. They thought that probably the birds had found some food in the forest, which they were pecking. So, they went about their search without minding the birds.

Chapter Thirteen

For three days, birds and men searched for the two flight recorders without finding any. For both birds and men, the search was tedious, arduous and tiring. Every day, the birds went into the forest surrounding the crashed aircraft looking for the flight recorders in the morning and did not return to the savannah until evening. If they had known the aircraft's path of flight, they would have concentrated their search for the aircraft along the path and perhaps made rapid progress thereby. But because they did not know the path of flight, they had to cover the forest surrounding the crash scene equally.

The forest the birds thought they knew, they found out they did not know with the intimacy they supposed. This made some of the birds to think they might not know the sky the way they thought they knew it since they had not searched it the way they were now searching the forest. The forest was full of wild life and strange landscapes they had never seen. They came across snakes, hares, antelopes, wild goats, worms and monkeys they did not know existed. A bird seeing a snake coiled up under a shrub thinking it was one of the flight recorders, pecked it and was smitten to death.

'Before you peck anything, look well,' the Lone Piper cautioned, looking sadly at the bird that had been smitten to death.

'The forest is so full of life that it appears there are no empty spaces in it,' said Longneck, 'and most of this life is deadly. The forest is mined with deadly animals; so inside it, we all have to pick our steps carefully.'

They came across thickets that looked like living forest houses of men. They saw barren patches of land said to be the former dwelling places of forest spirits. In one of these barren patches of land, a pillar of water that was to appear again and again to the Lone Piper, stood in midair before the Lone Piper. He called the pillar of water *the child of succour*. The pillar of water was soon replaced by a pillar of fire, which the Piper saw as a victim of the crash all in fire trying to flee into the pillar of water that had disappeared. The pillar of fire was replaced by a pillar of ashes, which the Lone Piper said was the ashes of the pillar of fire. He called the pillar of ashes *the ghost and child of sorrow of the crash*.

Of the three filmy pillars that stood before the Lone Piper by the barren ground, the pillar of ashes stayed so long that it may not be said to be a phantom, but a material form. Wherever he turned, it hung before his vision neither seeking his sympathy nor to frighten him. The Lone Piper began to sing:

> Below my nest, an owl all of fire
> Hung flaring and twinkling
> Like a million glow worms
> *Child of sorrow* you are like
> The glow worms beneath my nest

We have gone beyond mourning
To celebrating misery.
The ears of the forest are tired of
hearing cries

Saliva in the mouth has become tears
Tears in the eyes are burning like fire
That will eat the eyes and the cheeks
The air wears tears like the grass wears
dew

We have all lost the comfort of fear
And the joy of tears
Because misery is no longer a visitor
It is now the next neighbour
So, I look at you today
Without the fear and sadness of
yesterday.

The pillar of ashes disappeared from the vision of
the Lone Piper as he sang. The birds ferreting for
the flight recorders all stopped rooting for the
recorders absorbed by the Piper's melody. But it was
not only the birds that were absorbed by the melody.
The men searching for the recorders with the birds
were too. They listened to the sweet melody of the
Piper not knowing what the Piper's song was saying,
but enjoying it more than the birds who knew what
it was saying.

When the Piper stopped piping, some of the
birds began to search for the recorders again. But
others did not.

'Really I can't see why the Lone Piper is so
insistent the flight recorders must be found,' said a

bird yet to resume searching for the recorders. 'So far, the search for the recorders has cost us the life of a bird and I am yet to see a single benefit we have gotten from the search.'

'Yes, it has cost us the life of a bird and no bird knows what is coming next,' said another bird. 'Look at the forest; it seems to be smiling evilly at us.'

'Demons keep whispering into my ears and I don't like what they are saying,' said Beakybeaky. 'Though the Lone Piper did not tell us what he saw or heard before he started piping, what he said in his song and the expression on his face while he was piping told me that he had either seen or heard something terrible in this forest.'

'The Lone Piper will say not to look for the recorders will cost us more,' said a bird.

'There is no benefit in this search,' murmured Beakybeaky

'Sweat should buy sweet,' groaned Ruddycheeks.

'Beakybeaky, you can't say no benefit has come out of this search,' said Clawface, a grave-looking bird not given to much speech. He has been listening to the birds protesting the search without saying anything, but now felt he must say something to help sustain the search he did not want abandoned. 'You now know the forest more than you had ever known it and that is benefit.'

'So, it is benefit to know more horror?' asked Beakybeaky.

'Yes, it is a lot of benefit. When you meet horror, you know that life is a dying pleasure and not a living joy; you know life as a living mess, not a dying sorrow.

'We are exercising our legs on the ground as we exercise our wings in the air,' said another bird close by. 'This to me is benefit.'

'That is a great benefit,' said Clawface. 'If our war with humans leaves the sky for a ground war, we can outrun them on earth as we outfly them in the sky.'

'I believe the flight recorders will never be found by either bird or man,' said a bird. 'So, we are only wasting our time and punishing ourselves searching for the recorders in a treacherous forest like this. I believe even the *Heart of the birds* has not thought of this possibility. He is only thinking of the possibility of finding the recorders.'

'It seems there are many things the *Heart of the birds* has not thought of. Let's sound him out on some of these things to know if our suspicion is right,' said Beakybeaky.

Beakybeaky, Ruddycheeks and three *minta* birds hopped to where the Lone Piper was.

'We have been thinking of many things,' said Beakybeaky when they got to the Lone Piper.

'So long as what you have been thinking of does not include our abandoning the search for the flight recorders, I have nothing against it,' said the Lone Piper.

'Unfortunately, it is mostly about it,' said a *minta* bird. 'But hear us first before you decide.'

'Filifili!' exclaimed the Lone Piper.

'Yes,' said the *minta* bird.

'Remember you were one of the *minta* birds that excreted in the crashed aircraft lying all over this forest in ruins,' said the Lone Piper, curving his right wing to express by action what he was saying.

'Surely, I was.'

'If the flight recorders are found by human beings and analysed to a point it is known the engines of the aircraft failed because birds excreted into them, you stand accused than other birds around here,' said the Lone Piper.

'Am I being blackmailed?' asked the *minta* bird.

'No one is blackmailing you,' said the Lone Piper. 'If there was such intention, we won't be searching for the recorders the way we are doing now. I only want you to appreciate the great service you rendered in bringing down that accursed aircraft and the great service you are required to render to keep the matter secret.'

'That is very soothing,' said Beakybeaky. 'But I think you should still hear certain views on this search.'

'Sometimes, there is as much harm in listening as in doing what you are requested to do. For if you had not listened, you won't have been persuaded to do what you desire not to do,' said the Lone Piper.

'*Will*, you will always have the *will* not to be persuaded to do what you desire not,' said Beakybeaky.

'If I have a weak *will* to be persuaded to listen, I will have a weak one to be persuaded to do what is desired of me.'

'I don't think it is a weakness of *will* to be persuaded to listen. Rather it is a demonstration of strength and courage. It is cowardice to refuse to listen out of fear that you may be persuaded to do what you want not. Strength of *will* is shown by listening and refusing to do what you don't want to.'

'You are very right,' said the Lone Piper. 'I am listening. What are these views you talk of?'

'Some birds think the flight recorders will never be found by birds or by men and therefore we are labouring to nothing,' said Beakybeaky.

There was nothing on the face of the Lone Piper to tell Beakybeaky what he thought of what he said.

'What is the other view?' asked the Lone Piper.

'Some birds think so far there is only labour and death in this search; no benefit,' said Beakybeaky.

'What are the other views?'

'There are no more views. It is your own view on these views that is now being awaited.'

'I am happy we are using our heads like birds,' said the Lone Piper. 'That way we will remain ahead of the gentiles in the business of life. I have also thought of these things and thought of calling off the hunt for the flight recorders, but when I see human beings still searching for the recorders and remember the search for the recorders is part of our campaign to kill those killing us, I refrained from calling off the search. Brassfeathers, we have to persevere. There has never been any heroic feat that was not paid for with perseverance. Perseverance in every aspect of this fight is what is needed to have the last laugh in it, brassfeathers.'

'What am I seeing under that shock of leaves there?' said Clawface who had been looking at something under a thick shrub ahead of him while the Lone Piper was speaking.

The other birds followed the direction of his eyes and also saw what he had seen. They all hurried to the shrub and found the thing to be mushrooms they had never seen. The mushrooms had a rosy colour and emitted a sweet smell.

'Ruddycheeks, where are you?' Beakybeaky called out. 'You were the one that was saying sweat should buy sweet. 'Here is the sweet your sweat has bought.'

The Lone Piper pecked one of the mushrooms and the taste of it in his mouth was so exhilarating as to intoxicate. Almost at once he felt his limbs becoming stronger and yet more pliable. Almost involuntarily he flapped his wings as if he wanted to fly. Immediately he summoned other birds that were at different parts of the forest searching for the flight recorders to assemble by the mushrooms. Soon the forest by the mushrooms was swarming with birds.

'We have never seen this type of mushrooms before,' said the Lone Piper. 'From the taste of the mushrooms and the instant effect they have on me, I believe they have medicinal properties. I believe they are a tonic, a sort of elixir of life. Because there is no space for all bird to taste the mushrooms at once, the few birds at the centre with me can peck the *limb-tonic*. After tasting the elixir, they would make way for other birds to also have a taste.'

All the birds standing near the Lone Piper pecked the mushrooms and after them, other birds. Each bird was thrilled by the taste of the mushrooms and their instant effect on his wellbeing. Like the Lone Piper, many birds after pecking the mushrooms flapped their wings involuntarily as if they would fly.

'If we needed a tonic for flight, we have found one,' said the Lone Piper. 'If we needed an elixir for life, this is it. Woe to those who trifle with us! We may not have found any of the flight recorders, but we have found something that gives power to our limbs. With power in our limbs, we can chase away or even kill the lousy humans searching for the *secret-keepers* so that if we don't find them, they don't either.'

'The *Heart of the birds* has spoken cried many voices together.

At once, the birds descended on the three men searching for the recorders and started pecking them viciously. Screaming in fear and shock, the men fled to where their helicopter was, pursued by the birds. Longneck kept pecking the eyes of the man he was attacking until he removed his two eyes. Blind, the man blundered into a tree and fell down screaming. The other two men who were able to make it to the helicopter were too scared to come to the rescue of their fallen companion whom the birds had all descended on. In their fear, the two men by the helicopter forgot the fallen man was their pilot and without him, they could not fly the helicopter to safety.

Chapter Fourteen

The birds did not leave the man on the ground until it was clear to them that he was dead. They looked in the direction of the helicopter and were surprised to see it still where it landed. They had been so obsessed with killing the man they had brought down that they had thought the other two had flown away in the helicopter. Seeing the helicopter still where it was, they were happy and flew towards it.

But the two men were not in the helicopter. Seeing that their companion would certainly be killed by the birds and that none of them could fly the helicopter, they fled on foot knowing the birds would descend on them after they had killed their companion. It was a difficult flight for the two men. One of them had lost an eye in the attack and the other eye that could see was bleeding. So he had to be assisted in the flight by the man who could see well. Holding the half-blind man by the hand, the man who could see blundered through the forest, scarcely knowing the direction they were fleeing. As he fled, his right leg kicked against something hard and he fell down taking the man he was holding with him. When he looked to see what he had stumbled on, behold it was the black box. Not far away from it was the cockpit recorder.

'Impossible!' exclaimed the man who could see.

'It is more than impossible. Birds attacking human beings like this!' whined the half-blind man who was yet to see the two flight recorders. 'It is too strange to contemplate.'

'That is not the impossible thing I am talking about,' said the man who could see. 'I am talking about the flight recorders we could not see with our eyes all these days only for us to stumble on them when we are chased by birds. Look at the two flight recorders before you. It was the black box I stumbled on and that was what brought us down.'

'You don't mean it,' groaned the half-blind man trying to see the two flight recorders with his blurred vision.

'I can't joke over a matter like that in our condition, can I?'

At last, the half-blind man was able to make out the black box and cockpit voice recorder with his blurred one eye. 'It cannot be true,' he muttered gaping at the black box and the cockpit recorder, stunned.

The man who could see was also staring vacantly at the flight recorders. In quick succession, two strange things had happened to them that he thought he must be dreaming. First, without provocation and without warning, they had been attacked by birds, which most likely, had killed one of them. Secondly, they were fleeing from the birds when they stumbled on the flight recorders they were almost giving up the search for. He was a superstitious man who found supernatural explanations for strange happenings like these. It was now clear to him that they had a warning of the birds' attack before it happened, but they did not heed the warning. That they could not easily find aviation fuel to fuel the helicopter was a persuasion they should not come for the search, but they were too *civilised* to hearken to the persuasion. Now they were paying for their *civilization*.

The half-blind man, wracked by pain in his removed eye and stunned by surprise at finding the two flight recorders the way they did, could neither think nor talk.

'The very recorders we have spent weeks searching for chose to show themselves only when we are chased by birds,' said the man who could see. 'No doubt, there are witches in this forest.'

The half-blind man said nothing.

'We cannot carry these recorders and flee the forest the way we are,' said the man who could see. 'The best thing is to drag ourselves and the recorders to a hiding place from where we can seek help. I am sure when these birds are through with Bakofe, they would come after us.'

'There is little or nothing that I can do,' mourned the half-blind man. 'They may as well come and finish me up.'

'Boro, do you think they will kill Bakofe?' the man who could see asked, rhetorically.

'Ojames, they have already killed him and they will kill us if they find us,' said the half-blind man with levelled certitude.

'It is terrible!'

'Horrible is the word!'

'What!'

'Ghurr…mmm.'

'It is so unnatural and shocking; birds attacking people like honeybees? In fact, when we were first attacked, I thought we were being attacked by honeybees. It took me time to know we were attacked by birds,' said Ojames.

'We humans have done strange things,' groaned the half-blind man.

'So, we shouldn't be surprised to see strange things happening?' asked Ojames. 'I think even for beings that have shocked the world with their novelties, this attack is beyond what they may expect. What in your mind, do you think made the birds attack us? To my knowledge, we did not attack or even provoke them.'

That's what I can't understand,' said Boro. 'But certainly, there must be a reason for this attack. It was so vicious and I think vindictive. Well, you know I can't think well now; not with the wracking pain in my eyes.'

'For the past three days, the forest has been swarming with birds. What could have been bringing them to the forest in such numbers?' Ojames wondered aloud. 'If we must know why they attacked us, we must find out why they were in the forest in such numbers.'

'My eyes!' cried Boro under a stab of pain.

Ojames ran to him conscience-stricken. Stunned by the birds attack and shocked by finding the flight recorders the way they found them, he had not given to his injured companion the attention he deserved. Boro was lying on his back face-up. Ojames raised his head and placed it on his thigh. Using a leave, he cleaned the blood still oozing from the empty socket of the plucked eye and tried soothing the half-blind man.

'Oh Bakofe,' cried Ojames as he cleaned Boro and soothed him at the same time. 'This is all very horrible. To be pecked and clawed to death by birds.'

'They would do the same thing to us if they find us,' groaned Boro.

'Rather than sit here talking, let me look for where we can hide before these wild birds come looking for us,' said Ojames, gently removing his companion's head on his thigh and standing up to look for a hiding place. Not far from where they were, he saw a thicket that would completely conceal them from the birds. He quickly ferried Boro and the flight recorders into the thicket. Inside the thicket, he felt his pockets for his mobile phone and was happy to find it in his hip pocket. In his flight, he had forgotten about it completely and wouldn't have been surprised if it had fallen off. He brought out the phone and to his further relief, there was service where they were. He began dialling their office for help.

The birds not finding the two men in the helicopter knew they had fled. They descended on the helicopter and began pecking and clawing gadgets in the cockpit.

After a while, the Lone Piper said, 'instead of seeking to wreak the helicopter, let's pursue these cowards and see if we can finish them the way we finished their companion. We can return to the helicopter later.'

They abandoned wreaking the helicopter and set off after the men.

Chapter Fifteen

The birds led by the Lone Piper flew to and fro looking for the two men that survived the attack. The first time the two men in the thicket saw them, Ojames almost panicked. The sight of the birds flying over the thicket, their eyes boring into the forest, apparently looking for them was so unnatural and scary. But they were so well concealed by the thicket that the birds could not see them. Boro instead of being afraid was angry. If only he had his gun with him and could see. He would have come out of the thicket and blasted these filthy creatures hovering in the sky to death. He had a habit of gnashing his teeth whenever he was very angry. Now he was gnashing his teeth. To the relief of Ojames, the birds flew past the thicket without seeing them.

'What is the matter?' Ojames asked Boro who was still gnashing his teeth in impotent anger.

'Those philistines!' he swore. 'I wish I have my gun with me. I would have blasted them out of the sky for good.'

'But you don't have your gun and you can barely see.'

'Yes, I can barely see and I am in pain,' said Boro, gnashing his teeth. 'But I wish I have my gun with me. Oh...It is so annoying.'

'Even with a good sight, birds in the air are not an easy target. They may look like a band; but the moment you pull the trigger, they dissolve into their tiny units and your bullet would roam the sky without what to eat. You would end up wasting your bullet without hitting a bird. After wasting your bullet without benefit, these birds would waste you.'

'When the leper was told God would deal with him, he asked, if God can do anything worse than what he has already done. These birds have already wasted me.'

'I mean what remains of you.'

'Without my eyes, what remains of me is not much,' snorted Boro. 'If I had my gun, I would have taught them a lesson they seem to have had no occasion of learning.'

'These birds look to me like they are beyond learning any lesson. They look like they have taken all the lessons life has to teach them and are out to teach others the lessons they had learned,' said Ojames.

'What have we done to them? Are they not satisfied they have killed Bakofe and removed my eye?' fumed Boro.

'Shii…' whispered Ojames. 'They are returning.'

Boro seething with rage tried to break cover and defy the birds, but Ojames held him down. Fortunately for Ojames, even when the angry man was well, he was much stronger than him.

Their eyes looking wild, the beaks of most of the birds were still covered with the blood of Bakofe as they flew over the thicket for the second time looking for the two men. The second time, they were pecking the forest with their eyes more methodically than before. In the thicket, Ojames was as still as a statue. The birds flew over them only to return for the third and last time. The last time, Boro sat with a resigned posture seeing the birds in the sky in a blurred, hazy fleet without a show of much emotion. But it was not because he had burned all the anger in him that he sat staring vacantly into the sky. He was in conflicting emotions. Ojames has been very kind to him. But for his help, he would have been killed by the birds like Bakofe. It was his help that brought him to the thicket they were inside. If he breaks cover and brings the birds upon them, he might be seen as doing so to make his companion lose his eyes as he had lost his, or even to be killed as he would certainly be killed. That would not be a good way to pay back a man who had saved his life. Saved his life? he wondered. For what? So that he and others would laugh at him? When he thought like this, there was a visible squeeze on his face as he tried to suppress an urge to shout. The second time the thought came to him and he saw an expression on Ojames' face that looked like he was sneering at him, he shouted. But luckily the birds were out of earshot.

Night was falling. The birds led by the Piper, not finding the two men, decided to return to their nests in Kirkina savannah for the night.

Again, Ojames reached for his phone to try to get Emihu his colleague in the office who he had been trying to get without success. In their office, Emihu was the most reliable man a person in distress could depend on for prompt action. Ojames had tried Emilu's number several times without getting him. Each time, he was told the number was switched off.

He must be either at a meeting or instructing some students, he thought. Because of his contributions, Emihu was always at one meeting or the other. Since he could not find Emihu, he had to call Guguma the head of the safety department. Guguma was a very disagreeable fellow. One dial and he found Guguma. This is life he thought. Whatever is of little value comes cheap. He told Guguma the misfortune they had suffered, but they had found the flight recorders.

At all times Guguma always seemed to care more about machines and instruments than human beings. Another man would have expressed shock that birds had attacked and killed a man and would have been full of sympathy for the injured and distressed men in the jungle; but not Guguma. By the time Ojames finished telling him the state of things in the jungle, he could sense that Guguma was more interested in the flight recorders and the safety of the abandoned helicopter than rescuing them from the forest.

'Where did you say you left the helicopter?' Guguma asked with a lot of concern in his voice.

'At the scene of the crash,' Ojames said with mounting irritation.

'Oh my God,' Guguma muttered at the other end.

Does he have God? wondered Ojames.

'What of the flight recorders; are they there with you?'

Ojames almost screamed at him. What was the matter with this man? He had just told him Bakofe had been killed by birds and Boro has lost an eye, but Guguma was not concerned with any of these misfortunes that had befallen them; instead, he was only concerned with a helicopter and the lousy recorders that got them into the mess. Surely, if Guguma continues like this, he would throw away the recorders and sneaked back to the helicopter and set it ablaze.

'Bakofe is dead and Boro is without an eye,' Ojames repeated, the words tumbling out of his mouth with a hiss.

'Oh, sorry about that,' said Guguma.

'Bastard,' Ojames swore, after switching off his cell phone. But for the fact that he was relying on Guguma, he would have cursed him on the phone, not minding that he was his senior in the office. Imagine the son of a bitch saying, *oh, sorry about that,* as if it was their misfortune alone and nothing of his. Well, he had to admit he could not afford to get mad at Guguma in the position he found himself now. He had to control himself until he gets out of the mess. Then he would give the misfortune of a bastard a piece of his mind. He switched on his cell phone again. After waiting for a while without Guguma calling him back, he called Guguma again. The phone rang for a long time before Guguma picked it.

'Who is that?'

'Ojames,' said the distressed man, struggling not to scream at Guguma.

'Yes, what do you want?'

'Have you forgotten we are in the forest without means of coming back to town?' Ojames asked, peeved beyond tolerance limits.

'Oh, I almost forgot,' exclaimed Guguma. 'You know the pressure of work in this office. But you can see it is getting dark. How can anyone find his way in a jungle at night?'

'What you are saying is that we should sleep in the jungle?'

'I have not said so.'

'It is difficult for anyone to find his way in the jungle at night, but it is not difficult for anyone to stay the night in the jungle,' Ojames said, ignoring what Guguma had said.

'Santos!' Ojames heard Guguma calling one of the pilots. Ojames and Boro have found the flight recorders, but...

Guguma was interrupted by shouts of jubilation. At last, the flight recorders had been found.

'But Bakofe who flew them to the forest seemed to be dead and...'

'Bakofe, dead?' Santos asked, interrupting Guguma again. 'What killed him?'

'Ojames said birds.'

'Birds, but that is ridiculous. How can birds kill a man?'

'I have been in this office with you; how am I supposed to know? Anyway, you will soon be in the jungle with Ojames and Boro; you can then ask them all the questions you want. Get two other boys and head to the forest and bring the recorders, the helicopter and the two men.'

Bakofe, dead? And killed by birds! This sounds like a bad dream from wonderland,' said Santos.

'It sure sounds like a nightmare,' murmured Guguma. 'Please, get cracking.'

'Do you know their location in the forest?' Santos asked.

'That is your own nightmare,' said Guguma. 'You will have to hunt for them in the forest and pray you don't blunder into the birds. From what I heard from Ojames, they are as nimble as rattlesnakes.'

'There is no humour in your joke, if what you said is meant to be a joke,' said Santos, looking sore.

'Why is everyone out of humour these days?' Guguma wondered aloud to himself. 'Well, about the location of Ojames and Boro, with your mobile phones, it should not be so difficult to track them.'

'I pray they are in a service area.'

'Ojames called me. So, they must be in a service area.'

There was silence. Ojames heard Santos walking out of the office, apparently to come and rescue them. He cut the connection. After cutting the connection, he remembered he did not have Santos' number and so could not have a tap on the progress of the rescue mission. He had to wait until Santos called him. He knew Guguma had Santos' number, but he could not bring himself to call Guguma again. He had had enough of him and would not speak to him again over their distress.

'Who is coming for us?' asked Boro.

"Santos; you don't have his number, do you?'

'I don't have it in my head, but I have it in my cell phone,' said Boro. 'But you know my set is with the birds.'

'It means we have to wait until Santos calls us. I hope he has my number.'

'If he does not, he would be dumb not to ask Guguma before he sets out.'

It was towards morning that the two men were rescued from the forest by Santos and his men.

Chapter Sixteen

The Lone Piper and other birds returned to the forest the following day to complete wreaking the helicopter and continue the search for the flight recorders only to find the helicopter was gone. They had not wreaked it to a point that it could not fly as they had thought. So, Santos and his men had used it to fly Ojames and Boro out of the forest.

'We fucked up yesterday,' lamented Longneck. 'We should have wrecked that helicopter completely. Now they have recovered it and would use it one day to fight us.'

'Well, it was not only the helicopter they carried away,' said Bignose; 'they also carried away the corpse of their brother that we left lying here. No bird would say that was not a good thing they did. I had been dreading the stench of his decaying body in the jungle while we searched for the flight recorders.'

All birds agreed it was good the corpse of the man they killed had been evacuated from the forest.

'They had taken him for burial in the ground,' said Longneck. 'There is no creature walking this earth as primitive as man. How do you dig the ground and put someone who you hope one day would rise up again and enjoy everlasting life or everlasting damnation?'

'As for everlasting damnation, there is no problem with that; he is already in everlasting damnation in the grave. The problem is everlasting life,' said Beakybeaky.

'But it might be possible that the man did not die as we thought,' said Ruddycheeks. 'Maybe he merely fainted and after we left, he regained consciousness and flew away with the helicopter.'

The possibility expressed by Ruddycheeks caused quite a stir among the birds.

'You mean it was possible we did not kill that man?' many voices asked together.

'It is possible.'

'How?'

'I don't know.'

'Then shut up. Stop visiting us with the misery in your heart.'

Though Ruddycheeks had been overwhelmed by the collective antagonism of the other birds to his suggestion, it was clear he had spoiled the happiness the birds came to the forest with by sowing seeds of doubt about the achievements of the previous day, which they were still gloating over.

'We might have fucked up things yesterday than we thought we advanced our cause,' murmured Longneck.

'We would be too severe on ourselves to say we fucked up yesterday,' said the Lone Piper. 'We did the best we could yesterday. You cannot win all battles. Even if we did not kill that man and I have no reason to believe we did not, the battle we lost yesterday is a minor one to the one we won. No human dares come to this forest again to look for the flight recorders.'

'That's very true,' said Bignose. 'We told them yesterday who owns the forest if before they didn't know.'

For a while, no bird spoke. The mind of the Lone Piper was engrossed by how they searched the forest for the two men the previous day after they had killed the man they brought down. It pained him the two men were able to escape from the forest without receiving the treatment they meted to their companion. He had no doubt the two men hid somewhere. Even when they were looking for them the previous day, he believed they would hide somewhere. He was familiar with the cunning ways man seeks to relieve himself of any labour. It was because he believed the two men had hidden somewhere that he was moving to and fro with the other birds searching for them. It was getting dark and the forest was too vast and full of thickets for them to cover the whole of it and smoke out the two men. But after they had given up the search and returned to the savannah, there was this particular thicket he developed a hunch the two men were hiding in. He thought of going back to the forest to investigate his hunch, but the day had been very tiresome and he was full of fatigue. Besides, even if he discovered the two men in the thicket, he alone could not fight them. And he could not wake up other birds to go back to the forest that night to deal with them. By going to the thicket, he might only end up making the men run away if that was where they were hiding and they become aware their hideout had been discovered. It was better he left the investigation of his hunch till morning when he and other birds would return to the forest to completely wreak the helicopter and continue the search for the flight recorders. In the morning, his hunch was less gripping than it was in the night probably because he felt that even if the men were hiding in the thicket he suspected, they were likely to have fled it by then. Still, he felt he should investigate the hunch for what it is worth.

'After we gave up the search for those men yesterday and returned to the savannah, there was this particular thicket we did not investigate that I had a hunch the men were hiding in,' he said. 'I thought of going off alone in the night to investigate my hunch, but when I remembered that I alone cannot kill them and I cannot wake all of you in the dead night to go off to the forest with me, I decided against the mission. Now that hunch has returned and I think we should investigate it.'

'We would be damned if your hunch comes true,' said Bignose

'We are already damned without it coming true,' said Ruddycheeks

Led by the Lone Piper, the birds flew to the thicket Ojames and Boro were hiding the previous evening. When they got to the thicket and entered it, they were shocked to see that it was where the two men were hiding; for evidence of their recent presence in the thicket was everywhere. There was no doubt that the Lone Piper was a wizard many birds thought.

'What luck, what misfortune!' exclaimed Longneck. 'To think we flew over this thicket almost three times without thinking of alighting on it and having a look makes me sick. Surely, they must have laughed at us and called us fools as we flew past them without knocking on their door.'

'Like you said, it was their luck and our misfortune,' said Bignose. 'We can't have all the luck in the world. Luck must go round because it is the thing that feeds every creature. We had the luck of finding those mushrooms, which made us fight like hungry lions. We cannot begrudge them their luck of us flying over them without seeing them.'

Some birds amazed, others angered by their discovery, they all flew back to continue the search for the flight recorders.

By afternoon of that day, unknown to the birds, the flight recorders they were still searching for in the forest were on their way to their manufacturers' laboratories Johnnycomb Avionics for decoding and analysis of their recordings of visual events and verbal communications in the cockpit during the flight – particularly the final moments of the flight before the crash. At Jonnycomb Avionics, all available data from the memories of the recorders were downloaded in a file and the file was taken to the National Transportation Safety Board for analysis. The black box recording contained approximately 27 hours of flight. The crash flight covered the last 42 minutes of this time.

Conversation in the cockpit environment recovered from the cockpit voice recorder showed the flight was uneventful until close to the crash. Analysis of the black box revealed that the two engines of the aircraft quitted within twenty seconds of each other. Examination of engine parts showed that the one-way-valves had been destroyed by a highly corrosive element, which had entered the engines and severely damaged them making them quit and fail one after the other. The corrosive element was taken to a laboratory and analysed, but its source and nature could not be determined.

After all the crash investigations, Homma, the owner of the airline gathered the senior staff of the airline and addressed them on aviation safety. 'Flying people in an aircraft is all about care and safety precautions taken on the ground,' he said. 'The marked difference between a car and an aircraft is that if a car develops mechanical problems on the road, the driver can safely park it off the road and repair it. Not so an aircraft. An airborne aircraft cannot be parked in the air for a mechanical problem to be rectified. It may cycle around in the air waiting for safe landing conditions in the airport, but it cannot park in the air to sort out a mechanical flaw. It has to be on the ground and by the time it reaches the ground, there would be no aircraft to be repaired. The evolution and sustenance of airline safety culture is critical to the survival of the industry. So also staff-risk perception of aviation hazards, willingness of staff to report safety hazards and action taken on identified hazards. We are giants in the industry and our reputation perhaps more than that of small players in the industry hang on our

record of flight safety. We have not been able to
determine the nature of the corrosive agent that
destroyed the two engines of this aircraft. What this
means is that we must all sit up and ensure that such
agent, whatever it is and wherever it came from
never finds its way into the engines of our aircrafts
again.'

Chapter Seventeen

A month after the crash, the Lone Piper and the other birds learned the two flight recorders had been recovered and had revealed the crash was caused by the failure of the aircraft's engines. The engines were corroded by an element whose nature had not been determined. The birds were elated. In the excitement that followed what they heard was a new reverence of the Lone Piper by the birds. The revelations of the flight recorders confirmed the fears of the Lone Piper which some of the birds had thought were baseless. More than before, every bird knew they must believe whatever he told them.

From now on, most of the birds thought, they had to rely more on the art of aerobatics to bring down an aircraft than on stealth. The art of aerobatics must be refined by constant practice to sublime perfection for them to get the kind of result they wanted. Every morning and afternoon there were flying trainings of other birds by the Lone Piper and Longneck who had mastered the art of aerobatics near perfection.

There are as many as 100,000 aerobatic manoeuvres,' said the Lone Piper.

'What!' the birds exclaimed in disbelief. There was a look of dismay on many faces.

'But all aerobatic manoeuvres have four basic foundation stones,' continued the Lone Piper, hurriedly. 'These are the loop, the roll, the stall-turn and the spin, which I have already taught you.'

The birds breathed a sigh of relief. Dismay was replaced by relief on many faces.

'The art of aerobatics is by far the most thrilling art in the world,' said Beakybeaky, looking at the Lone Piper admirably.

'That's true,' said the Lone Piper; 'and the good thing is that its perfection is within the reach of every bird. All a bird needs to perfect the art is practice, patience and perseverance against all odds.'

'Practice makes perfect,' said Clawface. 'Patience sustains efforts. Perseverance makes possible the impossible.'

'A bird is science,' said Longneck. 'His flight is art. We will combine the science of a bird and the art of his flight to fight and exclude from the skies the intruders.'

'Wings are our greatest assets,' said the Lone Piper. 'To get anywhere in life, we have to get the best from our wings – our greatest assets. Most birds know only how to get the best from their beaks. But even the pig which I consider the vilest animal knows how to get the best from his snout. How far a bird can express himself with his wings is how far he can distinguish himself from the pig. Let every bird sing a sweet melody to the genius of his wings and we shall all see the colour and scintillating drama we can stage in the sky.'

'Let every bird ignite the fire in his wings,' said Beakybeaky.

'Let every bird mobilise the genius of his wings,' said Bignose.

'To get the best from our wings, we must be involved in contest flying,' said the Lone Piper. 'It is full of pressure and anxiety, but in the end, it helps more than solo flying. If you can do well in contest flying, you will do well in the coming aerial combat.'

'We have talked,' said Longneck. 'But talking is a drone. It is action that is the bee that gathers the pollen that pollinates the flower. Talking does not hatch eggs. It is the action of incubation that hatches eggs. Let's have some action now.'

The birds all poised themselves for flight.

'Shrrrr....shiii ...quuip...' sounded the Lone Piper.

The birds shot into the sky, soaring, soaring, soaring into the cumulus clouds; beyond the cumulus clouds, farther, farther, farther. By a common will among them, they simultaneously spun in their flight paths, looped, stall-turned in different directions; then flick-rolled wingtip down, producing intricate patterns of indescribable grandeur in the sky. From the ground, it was a breathtaking sight. The sky was full of colour and drama hitherto unseen and unthinkable. The way, they flew into the sky, the birds in wondrous formations descended on the savannah.

'We can all refine this performance with practice,' said the Lone Piper, after they had rested. 'With time, you will find that when you go into a hyper spin, gravity loses its hold on you. What we need to concentrate on in future is precision flying. Precision flying may not be critical in an aerial ballet such as the one we had just had. But in aerial combat, it makes the difference between defeat and victory.'

As much as the Lone Piper taught the birds, he made them understand that no one can teach the fine art of aerobatics. Every bird must teach himself by constant practice, which makes perfect. Most of flight trainings were in the morning. In the evening, more *minta* birds went to more airports and as many aircrafts as they found with uncovered engines, they excreted into them. For close to nine months, the birds scanned the skies for a crashing aircraft, and combed the forest for a crashed aircraft, but saw none and found none.

There was agitation and restiveness in the savannah. Flying had become leisure to most birds and they were now more in the air than before. This led to an unprecedented traffic in the sky. Two birds flying at the speed of sound had collided and died. The birds were complaining that they were colliding with each other because more flying space they would have had had been taken over by aircrafts. One afternoon, the Lone Piper landed on *the mountain of blood* and played this tune on his pipe:

We have damned them with our anuses
But they refused to be damned
We must damn them with our wings
Our beaks are itching to peck metals in the air

Give wings to the wind
And give wind to wings
Vengeance is the raised wing of justice

Gleaming and hissing in the sun
Rolling like a spin and looping like a
loop

Itching to find the heart of a whirlybird
They have sowed bitterness in the wind
Dews of blood shall fall in the
morning.

The blood of dead birds and the tears
Of those left behind are dropping
From the sky in plum rivulets
Plummer than the plumage of a bird
They will reap blood where they sowed
blood

They sowed wind in the wind
Soon they will reap a whirlwind.
At an hour men expect the sun to rise
Blood, which they sowed in the wind
Would rise and blot out the sun
Where our wings stir and caress the
wind

The wings of whirlybirds tear the wind
to shreds

The wind is mutilated like a tattered rag
But the whirlybirds do not care
Pus from the reins of the mutilated
wind

Fills the sky with stench.
But the whirlybirds have no nose to
suffer the stench
The tears left behind by aircrafts
Is making birds to slip
In their paths of flight

Whirlybirds have taken over
Paths of flight left behind
For birds by their ancestors
We must claim back what is ours
Tiny insects crowded out of the air
Are now refugees on land
They are looking up to us
To recover their heritage for them.

Chapter Eighteen

For over a year, the birds continued their flight training, continued to excrete in the engines of aircrafts that were uncovered, continued to listen for news of air-crash; watched out for plane crash in the forest, but heard nothing and saw nothing. The poison in the excreta of the *minta* birds seemed to have lost its sting. The birds became agitated.

The Lone Piper called a meeting on *the tree of decision*. Almost every bird attended the meeting knowing important issues would be discussed. Birds that could not attend because of sickness or some other inhibition asked other birds to represent them and vote for them if voting was required on an issue. Because of the multitude of birds that turned up for the meeting, it could not be held on *the tree of decision,* but on the ground.

The Lone Piper stood at the centre of the birds and spoke for a long time on the need for action. In this life, only two things matter: Thought and action. Even truth and justice do not matter that much. 'Thought, thought and more thought is required of every bird. Action, action and more action is required of every bird,' he said. 'We have thought and we have acted on our thoughts. But more action is required. With the help of the *limb-tonic,* we have exercised our wings to outfly the fastest whirlybird. Our lungs – the engines of our planes can endure the torture of our lightning flights. But exclusion of humans from the skies – the object for which we have tortured ourselves to fly at the speed of light, is yet to be realized. The original reason we wanted to eject humans from the skies was that they are rupturing the wind with their aircrafts and dropping human flu on the savannah from their aircrafts. This reason remains valid. But there is a new reason. Because birds can now fly at the speed of light, flying has become leisure instead of labour. Most of the time now, many birds are in the air enjoying the cherished pastime of flying. This has increased traffic in the air. There is scarcely enough sky for birds to fly and if aeroplanes will continue to fly, there will be many air-crashes between birds and aircrafts, between aircrafts and aircrafts and even between birds and birds. I don't care if aircraft and aircraft crash into each other. But I care when an aircraft and a bird crash and the bird is killed. I care when a bird and a bird collide. Planes are bigger and occupy more space in the sky. But birds are more in number. The big but fewer planes are pushing the smaller but more birds into less and less spaces in the skies where they keep colliding with each other. Recently, there have not been less than five deaths caused by birds crashing into each other in the air. Few fat aeroplanes are squeezing out many little birds out of the sky. This must stop. For this to stop, we must take action. Action, action, action is what is now required of every bird. Brassfeathers, we must strike or remained stricken the way we are.'

For a long time, the birds basked in what the Lone Piper had said. It was so enlivening and captivating. Even birds that were not so intelligent understood what he said. His speech seemed to have fused the birds into one mind that had only one thought in it: Bring down the whirlybirds.

Even as the birds thought of bringing down aircrafts, a low-flying aircraft flew over the savannah as if daring the birds to strike. Wind from the aircraft swayed trees, grasses and ruffled the feathers of birds.

'See what I am talking about!' cried the Lone Piper. 'Even on the ground we are not safe from the whirlybirds. Look at this one that just flew past. Can there be more provocation and intention to obliterate all birds by man than this?'

'No!' the birds cried in unison. The few birds that were not convinced of the need for a bird-strike were now convinced of its urgent imperative.

The Lone Piper sensing the belligerent mood among the birds seized his chance. 'To *the mountain of blood*,' he cooed. Woe to the next aircraft that would fly over this savannah.'

All the birds flew to *the mountain of blood* for the first attack.

Soon the sound of an approaching aircraft reached the birds on *the mountain of blood*. All birds poised for flight.

'Shrrrr.. .shiii …quuip…' sounded the Lone Piper when the aircraft came within a striking range. 'Woe to the whirlybirds!'

The birds shot into the sky, soaring, soaring, soaring into the cumulus clouds; beyond the cumulus clouds, farther, farther, farther; encircling the aircraft and obscuring it from view.

The pilot not expecting an attack, rolled the plane in a loop to avoid the birds, but the birds more skilful than the pilot in the art of aerobatics could not be shaken off. They rolled and looped with the aircraft, crowding closer on it until the pilot could no longer see the route ahead. The birds had dissolved into a wind shear that was rolling, looping and stall-turning against the aircraft rocking it violently. They could hear the passengers inside the aircraft screaming and shrieking as the pilot battled hopelessly to fly them to safety. They could see them shivering and cowering away from death which kept leaping towards them like a cat with nine legs. It thrilled them beyond measure to see creatures that had terrorised them all their lives whimpering with the least courage in the face of mortal danger. For about ten minutes, the pilot cycled round and round the savannah trying to shake off the birds and avoid a crash, but all in vain. The birds could see his face glistening with sweat; they could see his hands straining and pulling at different levers in the cockpit, but it was all in vain. The birds stuck to the aircraft like intent bugs blotting out the vision of the pilot and rocking the aircraft perilously. The pilot unable to manoeuvre the aircraft further, the aircraft finally crashed into the savannah not far away from *the mountain of blood*. When it finally nosed dived to crash, the birds that clung to the aircraft drifted apart the aircraft like parachuted pants and landed on *the mountain of blood* where they stood looking down at the carcass of the crashed plane and hearing the wailing of passengers that survived the crash.

The aircraft burst into flames moments after it crashed. As maimed people trapped in the burning aircraft wailed for help and struggled to crawl out of the raging inferno below the mountain, the Lone Piper began to pipe:

> Birds are friends and warm of heart
> But the greed and vanity of man
> Put to flight the warm hearts of birds
> Where the warm hearts used to be
> Cold hearts now perched, screeching
> Gobbling and feasting on the blood of
>   men
> Birds would now be a menace in the air
> Aircrafts would have to reckon with
> Before they set sail into the sky
> Birds have become clouds
> They have turned into storm
> Birds have become lightning
> They have turned into thunder
> Clouds are our friends
> We shall turn the clouds against the
>   rude beings
> The wind is our friend
> We shall turn the wind against the mort
>   beetles
> Thunder is our friend
> We shall turn thunder against the
>   gentiles
> We are not asking for the moon
> We are children of the sky where the
>   moon is

We are not asking for stars
Every night we sleep with the stars in
    our nests
We are asking for justice and regard
    among all creatures
The hyena was not meant for the aqua
    regions
Roamed by the crocodile and the shark
The hyena was meant for the rocky
    regions
Where he lives in the ancestral caves of
    his forbears
If the hyena is moved by gluttony to the
    river
He is courting the anger of the crocodile
    and the shark
Men stay on the ground with the mort
    beetle and the earthworm
Where you were meant to live as
    neighbours
The sky is for birds and insects
Greed is a basket no water can fill
Leave greed alone
Envy is a weevil that eats the bean that
    breeds it
Leave envy alone
Without greed and envy
The world will know peace again.

The birds listened to the song of the Piper with
kindness in their hearts and understanding in their
minds. But would men listen? Did they even

understand what the Lone Piper was saying? Making peace with the birds meant surrendering the skies to them. Could the greed and vanity of human beings make allowance for this? Would the greed of man not seek to evolve counter terrorism measures to meet the *terrorism* of the birds instead of allowing for a peaceful settlement of the dispute over the skies? the Lone Piper wondered. Many other birds wondered with him